TERRA FIRMA

TERRA FIRMA

Christiane Frenette

Translated by Sheila Fischman

CORMORANT BOOKS

The publisher gratefully acknowledges the support of the
Canada Council for the Arts and the Ontario Arts Council
for its publishing program. The publisher also
acknowledges the financial support of the Government of
Canada through the Book Publishing Industry Development
Program for its publishing activities.
The translator gratefully acknowledges the assistance of the
Canada Council for the Arts.

Printed and bound in Canada

Canadian Cataloguing in Publication Data
Frenette, Christiane, 1954-
[Terre ferme. English]
Terra firma

Translation of: La Terre ferme.
ISBN 1-896951-18-X
I. Fischman, Sheila II. Title. III. Terre ferme.
English.

CORMORANT BOOKS INC.
RR 1, Dunvegan, Ontario K0C 1J0

for Jacques Risler

CONTENTS

PART ONE

THE ARK AND THE RAFT

*What they know of the world
and of living is quite simply,
Mama died very early.*
— Louis Aragon

You have become a wave that's broken over the town, a murmuring beneath the leaves, a sadness deep in the eyes.

Onlookers on the docks pass binoculars back and forth, they raise their voices, scan the horizon, their hands shading their eyes. In the distance, coast guard vessels ply the river, helicopters fly over it. A brief news item, a disaster. Two teenage boys have headed out to sea on a makeshift raft. They left a message in which the words *leave, lie, worse, better* are repeated again and again.

Somewhere in the town, people are sitting around a table. They pass a crumpled letter back and forth, in silence. Now and then their eyes accuse, now and then they reassure. From time to time one of them rises, puts his arms around the mother's shoulders. Then they get up from the table, leaving at the centre of it, as if it were the centre of the world, the letter that is now a notice of disappearance.

A pain even sharper than that contained in the message rose in their veins when your raft was brought back to the dock. Silence flooded over them, each of them letting himself be devastated by a cry to which he couldn't give voice.

The landscape is triumphant in its light. This river makes everything unique: trees, pebbles, the expressions in people's eyes. Two names, two faces on the front page of the daily paper. You orchestrated your departure very well: the absence over the weekend, the raft no one knew about, the peaceful night, the cold. You were silent. You put the raft in the water as if you were performing some sacred act, as if you had to make up for all the rituals you'd never been taught. And then you seated yourselves back to back, leaning against one another. Turning your heads, you saw the bank of the river move away. Across the river, darkness, its texture and its muffled song. You thrust your hands into your coat pockets, where you'd stuffed photos, a piece of cloth that brought good luck, a tuft of your dog's hair. You felt as if these objects were warming your hands. You held them very tightly.

Who gave the signal? You slipped to the edge of the world. You didn't say anything, you didn't resist, didn't have even a hint of regret. You jumped. The river closed up again. There were no more stars, no galaxies, no frontiers. Only the ragged sound of the water and a colour in the east, very faint and very soft, which declared that nothing is ever finished.

Time seems suspended. On this October morning, a small and luminous town holds her breath and demands of her river that it spit out her children. Some have given in to the temptation to leave their quiet neighbourhoods and go back to the dock. Perhaps the end of the world will resemble this morning: trees trembling, geese flying over the sandbars, the blood slowing in our veins, no need to keep up the fire. Everything could fade away here, now, on these docks, these benches, and no one would feel that coming here had been pointless.

A truck roars to a start. Bystanders are beginning to leave. It's noon and life is reasserting itself. Each of them scans the horizon one last time, as if to salute you, then heads back home with his hands in his pockets.

A girl with long hair is wandering the streets of the town. Her coat collar is pulled up, her heels tap against the pavement; the girl walks slowly, cries silently. Doesn't know why. She moves, she scrutinizes other people's expressions, in vain; the pedestrians are blind and the street shatters in the sunlight with every clack of her heel.

The girl goes into a café. From the window she looks out at the world and its fury, which is going on without her. With hot chocolate in her cup, her hands wrapped around it for warmth, the girl is waiting for something to happen — for a bomb to go off, fragment the universe and put things back at its centre. She is waiting for a gaze to transfix her, for words to reach her, for a hand to rest on her head or shoulder. The girls who wait in the afternoon, sitting on benches in cafés, are goddesses but they aren't aware of it. They've forgotten that they have passed through time, they don't see the halo of light around them, exhausted as they are from spending thousands of years waiting in cafés.

Outside, the pulse of life goes on: men and women, embracing or hunted down, cars, movements, sounds clashing, as if numbing yourself could make up for what's missing.

The girl thinks about Noah, about the flood that swept over him, about the panic that shook the living. About the implacable law of two of every sort that would engulf the rest of humankind in an incredible trial by water.

Around her, the café customers tirelessly bring the conversation back to the two teenagers. Each of them bites into a precise explanation, sometimes sociological, sometimes psychological. The goddess listens as they get lost in conjecture. What do they know about the young men who walk the gangplank? About the irresistible urge that drives them out of the circus of everyday life? To understand, you must look for the fires that have burned everything, or perhaps not enough; you must seek out the places, the fountains, the murmur with which every cell, every fraction of the world reminds us that we are strangers. The girl can't see in the young men's action any specific expression of despair. As far as she's concerned, they got up abruptly, fists raised in the air, and chose to stop waiting, chose never again to sit at a café table. They've joined with the flood, and with those who refused to make their way to the ark. They preferred the wrath of God to any promise for the future.

The day's end muddles colours and faces. The girl gets up, puts on her coat and imagines doing it for the last time. The rustling of the cloth, the sudden weight on her shoulders, the collar to be pulled up, the belt to be knotted: ridiculous actions, protection against the cold, against the world. Suddenly your image comes to her. Your pallor, the seaweed wrapped around your wrists. The slight movement of your hair in the water.

She joins the little five o'clock crowd that's smothered by fatigue. On her way home she frequently looks up to heaven to catch the first signs of a flood.

While every night on the TV news a series of images flows by, while each item is forgotten on the spot, replaced immediately by the next one, while visions of horror — famines, earthquakes — fly past at a frantic speed, while we're getting used to massacres of all kinds, this town is obstinately refusing to move on to other matters.

The sandbars are surveyed, searched thoroughly. Every fault, every crevice, every spot on the landscape is examined systematically. Churches see their attendance increasing. People consult mediums who declare that the young men, injured but still alive, have taken shelter in a summer cottage and are waiting for help, which has the effect of rekindling the searches even though they're still ablaze. Some clairvoyants advance a more sombre version of the present: they see the boys drifting out towards the estuary. Others dare to put forward the grimly cynical theory of a scam. As if the boys, wanting to test how interested in them mankind might be, had written the message and launched the raft into the sea and now, holed up in some secret place, were astonished to weigh the significance of their disappearance. Or else they'd chosen this scenario the better to run away. For every speculation there's a taker.

As for the river, its response echoes the murmurs from town. It repeats what everyone knows but still suppresses: with every passing second, hope recedes. It has borne everything away, as usual. The bodies we ask it for have already been carried off, at arms' length, a good distance downriver from the little town. In fact other communities that are less affected, more like onlookers, some kilometres away, are beginning to keep an eye on their sandbars as well.

The two of you are about to become the object of a treasure hunt, a lost trophy to be brought back to town in triumph — one that would make heroes of those who found you, and bring them glory. Desperate as we are, we don't think of your flesh, disfigured, scraped and swollen, of your odour of salt and death. Your youth alone obsesses us, and finding you seems a way to exorcise what you've done, to prove that you weren't justified. For the time being, the river is still your ally.

She has cut your photo out of the paper and put it up on the fridge. Beside the others. Those from the last vacation, those of newborn puppies, adjacent to the notice about insurance-policy renewal and the next dentist appointment. For a few days now you've dominated that kitchen with your inordinate smiles, your easygoing appearance.

She's not your mother. She's someone else's.

She too was struck full in the face by the wave. A sort of rage took control of everything she did and said. She didn't cry, didn't tremble. Initially she was incredulous; then she looked at her own children one by one, thinking to herself that it could be him or her, that she could be that mother, stranded, devastated, clinging to the raft.

Here in her bright kitchen, trivial facts delight her: the phone rings, a glass of orange juice spills on the tablecloth, the squirrel appears at the window demanding its daily bread. The familiar reassuring chaos of her days returns every morning and covers the voices she doesn't want to hear: diseases that creep furtively into young bodies, accidents, violent acts, horrors — the whole menagerie that conceals itself no one knows where, and bides its time, waiting to stumble out and ambush some warm, living being.

In a teenagers' bedroom in another house in town she pictures a thin little woman wearing a flowered dress and sitting on the edge of a bed. Who isn't crying, isn't trembling either. She is studying, incredulously, the photos that cover your walls: idols who don't speak your language and whom you worship though you have no idea of the revolt that compels them to cry out, that gives them their furious expressions and makes them hold their arms out wide. Your arsenal of everyday objects — schoolbooks, dirty socks, rumpled clothing — litters the room and makes it look surprisingly arrogant.

A moment later, the little woman gets up and goes to lean out the window. More arrogant still are the day, the sky and the river in the distance, its profound respiration.

She's surviving. She will survive. In spite of herself. That's what this bedroom and this window declare. That's what her own rage confirms to her.

Her friends and family try to stand by her. They maintain that the worst is over. The worst, of course, being the precise moment when someone tears off her skin in one go, like a rabbit's, cuts out her tongue, gouges out her eyes. Afterwards, right afterwards, she has to busy herself with healing. They suggest that she think of your way of dying as something else: a dumb accident, a fatality due to speeding. They utter words that stand for the new shape of the future: mourning, acceptance, resignation, peace. She tries to resist but it's complicated. She has to understand, has to penetrate your secret. She's beginning to miss the first days of the disaster, when pain had abolished every thought, every question. Nothing but exposed flesh, hours in suspense, rare slumber aided by pills, faces without names, voices she heard but didn't listen to. Now ordinary days are trying to regain vigour, and the things that life consists of begin to scratch furiously at her wounds: hot coffee in the morning, the newspaper, birds at the feeder. The present, implacable, continues to ring out.

She touches your faces, frozen in the photo. In the kitchen, bright light. She shudders; her own world is intact. Fate has spared her; it wasn't her turn. Now she closes her eyes. The silhouette of the thin little woman in the flowered dress reappears, and the difference no longer exists. You, on the door of the fridge, know that compassion is the worst of all illusions.

A few days later they call off the official search. A cry of protest can be heard above the town. There's an attempt to put pressure on the officials. The ships sail back to their home ports; the helicopters disappear.

People find themselves alone, facing the river.

But not everything is hostile. The autumn, an exceptionally mild one, lingers on; a late-summer warmth persists, envelops the countryside. It's as if the days have stopped growing shorter, as if the leaves are clinging to the trees as they blaze; it never rains, the sun lays waste to any areas of shade.

People are living outside, walking, taking over the terraces, the parks. As if to tell you to hang in there, you aren't alone, you'll be saved, it's only a matter of time. Chests swell; people want to seem brave.

Young men in particular are the target of people's gazes. They try to understand your action through them. To foresee the flash, the moment when the sharp sound of the fracture would be heard. To track it down in the eyes of all the boys who lean against the walls and smoke, while away their time on the docks, board the bus. One Saturday they think they've found an answer in the expressions of two young men walking off the soccer field, dripping wet and muddy. In the soothing light of late afternoon these two boys, whose arms are too big for them, whose legs are too long, have their arms around each other's shoulders. A bitter defeat, the season's over. They're together. That's enough, because there'll be no follow-up to these events. That's enough to explain the emptiness, the absence that made them run, pant, sweat throughout the match; they tried, they feel they went as far as they could. But it wasn't enough. The ball got away, escaped, and they had to run, run, run. Now they're getting their breath back. Have their arms around each other's shoulders. It wouldn't take much for them to give in to tears. They're alone. But together.

The whole town remembers that late afternoon. The murmuring had ceased. Some very young children were venturing into streets that were empty of cars, under the gaze of mothers sitting on the sidewalks, holding before-dinner drinks. The sun made them squint. For a short time you deserted their memories. They reconciled themselves to the salt cry of the geese, the harsh blue of the river. No one felt like resisting any more. People were saying yes to frailty, to the forlorn splendour of autumn, to those things that, having given everything, were ending: trees, leaves, gardens. No one was expectant any more. Either for better or for worse.

It was at the end of that day, precisely at the end of that day, that autumn, the real thing, rainy and cold and dreary, settled in — at the very moment when the last sailboat coming into the marina brought back one of your caps.

In front of a mirror you're not anybody. Any more than you are at the bottom of a river. This morning, a wrinkle holds her glued to her reflection. Fatigue, the colour of her eyes which is fading from day to day, from week to week. Attrition and ruin. A kind of absent expression. This, she tells herself, is death, one more death.

The two of you are there, a hazy image, jarring, afloat in the depths of her mirror.

She's angry with you for having the audacity to do it, for not waiting to be sure that life had passed you by before you acted. Your lack of patience shocks her. Yet her own patience hasn't brought her all that much. She comes home to her apartment every evening, sets down on the table where she eats, alone, purse, keys, newspaper: the personal belongings of her orderly, absurd, tormented little life. No one else has come along, neither husband nor children. No one has filled the silence, emptied the pantry. Nothing is scattered around this place, there's no trace of any disorder to indicate blood heating inside veins.

Though she'd never admit it, she envies you.

She has never walked on the rocks beyond the allowed limit, or floored the accelerator of a car some rainy night, has never spent her rage hammering nails to build a raft. It hasn't even crossed her mind. The impulse, the driving force that frees you from the rough side of things, is something she has never felt. She has gone on, not suspecting that there can be such a thing as a premature exit, not knowing that it takes only a quick twist of the wrist for the hand holding the wheel to topple the tall grass by the side of the road, to bring the river over your head. Just like that.

But this morning you are deep in the depths of her mirror, little heroes of her dejection, with your wet hair plastered against your foreheads, with that faded glimmer in your eyes and, in particular, the subdued looks on your faces.

You are there, like a truth that is finally revealed.

At the mirror she pieces together who she'll be today: hair brushed, makeup, clothes, perfume. Theatre, heavy artillery. She still attracts stares on the street. She quickens her pace to keep the image evanescent, so others don't have time to study the bags under her eyes, the wrinkles, the cheeks that are starting to sag.

Her life is like a bunch of keys left behind in an underground parking garage where she dares not venture after midnight.

The geese have left the sandbars. The great familiar streak of white has melted in one night. The town sinks more heavily into dullness. There's rain, the wind blows constantly. November is finishing its destruction. The ground is strewn with leaves. The soul is disappearing from the light. People take refuge inside.

They aren't forgetting you. But it's different now. You're still there deep in everyone's eyes and in their voices; your image breathes onto the embers, trailing its sound of waves and birds. But they've stopped trying to understand in the same way, with the same frenzy, as they did at first. Each of them has diligently gone back to the hours that furrow their lives with useless actions. Each has returned to the well-ordered place he occupies on the third planet of the solar system, clinging with hands and feet to adjust to the spinning of earth on its axis, each of them resigned to revolving around the sun.

The current has washed your bodies out to sea. You've left the family.

But in the disorder of the world, something of you continues to float above this town. At night your shadows pass gently along the river. You won't be forgotten, they've promised you that, but the current is also strong on the side of the living. And if they haven't yet contemplated finding a final nesting place for you, it's because they still occasionally see someone with arms flung up to heaven, lingering on the shores.

You aren't ready either. For the time being you prefer the depths of a mirror, the fridge door in a bright kitchen, the eyes of a girl on the brink of the deluge.

In the town's schools and colleges, they didn't make a big fuss. A kind of fellowship kept the young people silent. A way of consenting to your absence, of letting themselves be carried along in your wake.

When the girl thinks about you, she imagines the two of you side by side on the edge of a cliff: entrenched on the last heights on earth not yet submerged by the flood, you watch as the ark moves away; suddenly one of you bursts into demented, devastated laughter that terrifies the survivors crammed onto the deck.

And sometimes, to put herself to sleep, she'll wrap herself in blankets, cover her head, curl up with pillows all around her and let herself drift on your raft, wanting nothing but sleep. At those times she thinks that it's something like happiness.

In class she always sits at the back. Doesn't talk, doesn't try to answer questions, doesn't ask any either, smiles rarely, turns in her assignments on time, all in her wobbly handwriting.

The girl tells herself that even if the sea is unleashed on the inside, there shouldn't be any waves on the outside. That the storm only concerns the person caught in it. That it's better to stay out of the way and, above all, not alarm those who proclaim that youth is a luminous age, that all doors open at once onto fabulous geographies.

For the time being she sees nothing but dark cloudbursts pelting down before her, nothing but doors that are more or less open onto alleys, or that keep slamming in the wind.

There is no consolation.

She doesn't even know what it is that clashes. She's tried to find reasons. Has delved into childhood. Found there the same silence, the same immobility on the part of the world — a sort of quiet sorrow, conventional, with no tragedies, no ill treatment. Nothing that burns or warms. The very first version of dissatisfaction.

Friendship can't comfort her. Though there are some who are tracking her mystery, extending their hands. She recognizes the signs of affection she can read in their eyes, but she never lets herself give in to them; always gives halfway responses to the fervour of others. She's not to be seen among the noisy groups moving from place to place on Saturday night, doesn't spend hours on the phone, doesn't appear in any group photos at the end of the school year.

Certain impulses are beyond her strength.

One day, the bus she was on came to a stop in front of a Victorian house in the old part of town. At the side of the house two girls her age, dressed in white, were sitting on a blanket. Around them, the explosive green of grass and foliage. The girls, sitting very close to one another, were talking with their heads slightly bent, and smiling. She wondered what century she should have been born into.

Of love, she has known the first stammerings. Has known since childhood, instinctively, that there is no grand fusion. That it's not from love that redemption will come. But at least it makes the earth move under her feet, passes through her skin, touches great areas of darkness left vacant when childhood departs.

Boys hover around her like circus performers around the ring. Their flamboyant outfits, their cleverness, their music don't touch her. She can make out only their white eyes, the eyes of young wolves going round and round, a circular movement that always brings them back to where they started.

As a child, she thought she'd had the revelation of her life. That's the truth she clings to, tries to be loyal to: she's six or seven years old at most. June. Colours everywhere. A bright dress with a silk butterfly on it. Hair pulled back. The motion of the little dress. Muscles that move. The wind. She goes home by way of a yard, a narrow passage between two buildings, comes out into a street. Beside the house she lives in, two immense trees. She stops breathing. In a fraction of a second, she knows. That her whole life will be never be anything more than a little girl's superhuman effort to get herself moving, to keep in step. That what doesn't move is like these trees: immense. That every day she'll have to stoke the fire, tend to aching feet, hoist her baggage onto her back. That the worst fate is that of the trees frozen in the light.

Something will certainly happen, will stir slowly at first, then unfold, shake out its creases. Or it will roar, shatter, devastate everything it encounters. Or else nothing will happen. The usual course of the blood in her arteries will remain the only movement in her days.

To let herself drown, to flounder. Isn't there any place where she wouldn't have to choose? Only let herself glide along the silky side of the world. Without effort. Won't someone come along to lead her into her own motion? No longer have to choose. Effortless. Perhaps it's better to get used to it now; the world will never be equal to the task. The air in that place is so rare, so rare.

A tired young goddess walks across town every morning. Crosses it again in the opposite direction at night. Hugs the walls of a school as if they were precipices. Sits in a dingy, bustling cafeteria. Runs her hand through her hair. A young goddess who has no memory, to whom the gods have not transmitted the ancient knowledge. A girl who has nothing to question: the sky is closed to her, the present mute.

Written in felt pen on her backpack, the only question that matters: What time is the Big Bang?

Finally, snow falls on the town. Delicate wet snow that stays on the ground for just a few days but brings winter back. Soon they'll be cut off from the river by ice that covers the sandbars and extends some distance into the water. A barrier between the town and the two of you. Though they've finally resigned themselves to your disappearance, they aren't used to your absence yet and the river bordering the town has become a sacred site, a tomb, the only place where your absence can still be felt.

They are building your legend.

Some, more down-to-earth, fear an undertow. They dread the copycat effect, the way an act like yours may influence other teens who are tempted to follow your example. Psychologists and social workers take matters in hand. There's a rush to open youth centres in parts of town where there are none; experts track distress hidden deep in people's eyes. People are astounded, she doesn't hide away. She laughs hard, plays pool, sips a Coke or a beer. People throw an arm around her, rest a hand on her thigh. She has her ears and one nostril pierced, a black line under her eyes. She doesn't stand out.

And so people suspect that it wasn't a familiar distress that drove you out to sea. But they don't know what force it was that seized you bodily, what spell it was that wiped out fear, transformed it into a kind of definitive courage, they don't know what hands held yours until the end.

On the door of the fridge your photo continues to mark the time. She feels guilty. Thinks often about the mother who had to reconcile herself to tidying your bedroom, shutting the door and turning the room into a sanctuary she avoids entering. Or perhaps it's crossed her mind to sell the house. Which is what *she* would do.

Every morning, when they've all left, it's the two of you she sees after she's performed the ritual you imposed on her: to check each of her children's bedrooms, not touching anything, not prying into secrets, only sniffing their warmth, like an animal, in the shambles of objects and unmade beds. Suspecting the unforeseeable, guessing at what could become unbearable, having a premonition about the building of a raft.

Then she goes downstairs, sits at the table still adrift in breakfast aromas. Arrogantly, as if to give herself momentum, she looks straight into your eyes and recalls that here, where she lives, people eat, bring to their mouths bread, fruit. They make an effort. Or at least they still think they do.

Sometimes she speaks to the two of you out loud. Tries to persuade you to stay. She orders you, for instance, to look out the window; describes, as if you were blind, the landscape, frozen now at the beginning of winter, the desolation of the garden, that mixture of November and snow, the low level of light, the bareness. Then, when you've seen it all, smelled it all, she forces you to come back to this kitchen, to this table, to the pitcher of orange juice. Slowly she pours a glass, never taking her eyes off you. That's what you need to hold onto: oranges that have travelled thousands of kilometres — a whole continent — to end up on this table on this exhausted November morning and grasp some human beings by the throat. The taste of sugar, the smell, the sun in the glass, everything that's soft and mellow, that comes from somewhere else, from another world, rushes into them to keep them alive.

After this kind of harangue she usually cries and asks your forgiveness for going so far. She becomes prey to remorse. And then she goes to the fridge, apologizes for never having known the sensation of icy water on her body, to say nothing of the breath of air you know to be your last. Apologizes for knowing nothing but this house that's like a beating heart, where the unfettered pulsations of a few lives clinging to a raft are stirring.

And in this kitchen that in the morning, after her family has left, resembles a battlefield deserted by its combatants, the poor light of this late November day leaves her unable to speak or to move.

The arrival of December poses a moral problem for the town's business people and residents. How can they not give in to the frenzy of Christmas? They're uncomfortable at the prospect of decorating store windows or house fronts. The glittering lights, garlands, children's laughter, handshakes, good wishes become so many affronts signifying that you're no longer important, that along with the river the devil has carried you away. As if the town weren't respecting its mourning period to the very end.

That's no way to behave.

In the stores, sales don't take off as they usually do. Merchants are nervous. A few of them decorate their windows, discreetly. Instinctively, customers go to those shops. Other stores follow, then all the rest. And finally the streets, houses, even the churches.

People explain that they need a break to get through the winter, just a little pause, a month at the very most, that afterwards you'll resume your places, that the town will respect its mourning, impeccably, up until the statutory date provided for by law. They beg you to understand. The town doesn't want to provoke the anger of its young gods.

The river, for its part, settles quietly into its winter shackles. Stripped of its birds, deprived of its sandbars, cut off from humans. Merely a pause. A brief pause.

Now all three of you are in a painting. You two in the background, she in front. A moving picture, a mirror, every morning at a set time. You've ignited a subdued wish in her: to connect with your beauty.

A halo of light surrounds her. An eagerness has taken hold of her. An impudent, mocking expression has become ingrained in her features. People think she's beautiful.

She's no longer alone.

Since you've been there, she's been able to shed something heavy. As if you were now carrying her bags, as if you'd come to lighten her way.

She has started swimming. Goes to different pools several times a week. Throws herself in the water the way one throws oneself off a bridge or a raft. A question of learning how, of maintaining the elegance of the movement; then she swims lengths, more and more of them, often demanding more than she can give. Once she's reached the ultimate limit, she lets herself float on her back, eyes closed, offering herself to the tumult of muscles, blood, heart, all recovering from their turmoil. She listens to her breath as it calms down. She becomes light, her body open, in the middle of the sea. Without memory. Here she is merely a rock that has fallen to the bottom of the water. The part that's floating is another part of herself, the one reflected in the mirror each morning. That transparent part expects nothing, never feels pain, merges with the turquoise of the pool.

She walks home along the noisiest streets, burrows into the heart of the small crowd excited by Christmas preparations. She's cold, hurries on. In half an hour the few kilometres she adds to those she's swum will induce what she wants most: a deep, dreamless sleep until morning. A sleep in which she'll lose the notion of the empty and very precisely measurable space between herself and the edge of the bed.

You respect the respite. Christmas is nearly here. You've withdrawn discreetly. You let them give in to their excitement, to coloured gift wrap, to the warm aroma of cinnamon and spice. You let them persuade themselves that they're together; that they're reinventing the world in a small provincial town built on the jagged coastline of a broad and ageless river that runs to the sea; that in the red flames they are once more forging a humanity that will inscribe their names in time, and those of their sons; that they're finally able to give their voices a resonance that carries beyond this river. In lineups at supermarkets and banks they stand straight and proud, wish one another the best and the finest. Laugh loudly. Touch.

They aren't fooled, though. They know that it's just a remission, that the pain in their chests will return, that they'll begin again, defeated, to walk by themselves, silent, empty-armed, that the days will regain their insipid taste and that in the dreariness they'll continue to clench their fists in their pockets, that once again they'll feel infinitely small and abandoned as they burrow deep into their small town. Till the next respite.

As usual, she went to her room and shut herself inside early in the evening. Stayed there, lying on her back, holding a book, her eyes, her mind elsewhere. Didn't give in to sleep till very late.

Now the girl is dreaming that she's advancing very slowly in the river. Only those sensations associated with what she's doing are revealed sharply: the silt under her feet that seems to want to hold her to the ground, like a bloodsucker; the sound of cars on the road in the distance; the coolness of the water, on her ankles first, then on her knees; the hem of her dress, which grows heavier as she walks; the wind, the colour of the evening, the air that enters her lungs.

Suddenly she starts to shiver, an incredible shudder runs through her, making her tremble from head to toe. She stands rooted there, in water up to her waist, unable to go forward or back, imprisoned by her tremors.

She wakes in a sweat. She's still trembling. She's burning, then cold. Feels stunned, nauseated.

She gets up, goes to the bathroom, drinks some water, comes back staggering with dizziness. She pulls on wool socks, a sweater, snuggles under the blankets, goes on trembling for a long time, burning with fever.

In the morning, the tremors have stopped but the fever persists. Drowsily the girl reruns last night's dream. Scrutinizes the embroidery on the dress, the hair falling loose. Tries to see what position her arms are in. Hanging down? Is she swinging them? And her hands: closed? Open? It's like at the movies, a badly shot scene the viewer tries to make significant in spite of everything. The awkward, ridiculous heroine doesn't know what the scene is doing in the film, doesn't know how or why to play it.

On this day now beginning, a girl, pale and weakened, nestled under her blankets, returns to the beaches of childhood, steps onto the border of seaweed that she was forbidden to cross. Realizes she's never been on a boat, never crossed the river. Has never swum in it either. The river must be worshipped from afar. A cold master who crushes without touching. A law impossible to disobey. A secret declined.

A girl remembers nights of fever when she was a child huddled against her mother's body with a cold cloth on her forehead. A sick girl has got through the night. Without calling out. Without asking for cold water for her burning forehead.

Certain compromises imposed themselves. Every night just before midnight, there's a natural consensus: all the Christmas lights across town are turned off one after another.

It's around then too that a very cold wind sometimes gusts off the river, rushes into the streets, seeps under doors, into cracks, insinuates itself into every house, gently brushes sleeping bodies, wraps objects left where they fell for the night: open books, unfinished letters, rings, watches, medicine. A survival kit. Fragile, pathetic.

A wind that, unbeknownst to anyone, brings back for just a few moments the influence you have as young gods. You haven't been able to hold on. You haven't respected the break. You lack confidence: you need to check.

Now it's you who come, pleading, towards their strained faces that no sleep can ease. Now it's you who are overcome by fear.

And you don't place your cold hands on these living beings who are walled inside their dreams. Or on the blazing hot body of a girl who can't unknot her muscles so she can move them, even in her dreams.

At dawn you go back to the ice that's breaking up, to the river that teaches you everything, now that you've pierced its secret.

In the morning, when the girl bursts into the bright kitchen, she startles her mother, who thought she was alone in the house. The girl stands in the doorway, white, exhausted, with dark shadows under her eyes. Explains briefly that she was sick during the night, that she still feels weak, that she's going back to bed. Doesn't want anything. Disappears right away.

Now she's alone again in the middle of the kitchen. Had no time to ask a question. No one needs her. That's what the morning light on the kitchen walls tells her.

During the night, then, she was absent; she neither heard nor had any premonition of her daughter's drifting off course in the bedroom across the hall; didn't leave the closed circle of her own sleep; no tears, no moaning, no hand tugging at the covers came to pull her out of the place where every night she concocts her theatre of lies: stopping time, invincibility, happiness, compassion.

So here she is this morning, in this puppet-theatre decor, with the props needed for the daily presentation of the only show she believes she can control; here she is with her orange juice, with the squirrels at the window, with the whole battery of illusion; here she is, naked on the stage with her empty, ready-made lines that no spectator will hear.

For the time being, what matters is the girl who has just excluded her from her field of vision, who didn't ask to be rescued even when her fever was at its peak, who doesn't ask anyone for anything, especially her.

What matters is the thing that's dying, here in this kitchen and in the girl's bedroom upstairs.

What matter are her suddenly empty hands, this ridiculous business of being alone, standing in the middle of the kitchen, telling herself that her love has taken everything. That its walls are rough. That the time of distance and absence has arrived, with its horde of small torments: no longer touching her, no longer seeing the girl take shelter in her arms. And above all, being kept away from her pain, from anything inside her that struggles and wounds. During her periods of silence, her vacant stares, to feel her slip away from the easy days.

Something has just collapsed here, on the floor of this kitchen; something that will not be saved makes the ground open, creates a fault that will forever divide life in two: the time before and the time after. A bottomless breach in which to fling the emotional outbursts, the tears, the orange juice, the squirrels. Whatever is obsolete, superfluous, whatever bears the imprint of everything we are or will never be.

For a long time she stands there motionless, leaning against the refrigerator door, her head pressed against your photo, pretending not to feel your breath on the back of her neck.

Is it your breath that has finally spurred her to step over the fault and go upstairs to the girl's bedroom and gaze at her pale body, given over to sleep? To gaze as well at the slight movement of the sheets that rise and fall over her chest. Her love is a weighty presence in this bedroom. Like childhood. Like the sound of an ice floe tearing itself away from shore.

Winter is taking root. Gazes drift towards the river and its ridge of ice just before the wild blue in the distance. The town is gathering up its crumbs. The day before Christmas Eve. The final, desperate frenzy.

Everything is ready for the photo intended for posterity: snow falling gently, boots polished, furs brushed. Smiling children are held by the hand. It's nearly here. In a moment, everything that was finished, organized, wrapped weeks ago will exult, will crystallize long enough for a photo. They'll perform the big scene with conviction. They'll stick to their roles. They'll maintain the pause.

And all will go well. It has to go well. They've slaved to reach that point. They've assembled their families, stoked the fires in their fireplaces, poured wine into glasses.

Nothing else but these few hours of lying. Even that's a lot.

Deep in the mirror the two of you learn to be docile. You come when she asks you to, with that sweet manner that soothes her so. You see her bustling about, trying to extricate herself from her obsessions — like those three boxes in the closet that she reveres and loathes at the same time.

At first there was just one. Now there are three. Lined up at the very back, brightly coloured, impressive. She'd be hard-pressed to say when she made her first purchase. Twelve, thirteen, maybe fifteen years ago. A kind of collection. A keen interest that comes over her every year at this time. A way of marking her life.

She buys Christmas tree ornaments. Nothing run-of-the-mill, ordinary. Rare, unusual, most of them handmade. Not necessarily very expensive, with a clear preference for those found in antique stores or import shops.

At first she thought that it would bring good luck, that it would give her a lead in the race towards happiness, a way of summoning things, of making them come to her. Then, over time, her enthusiasm was blunted, but she still can't break off the ritual, lest she frighten what she is calling to, lest she attract disapproval. Those objects represent the ultimate award she'll give herself when life finally changes: there will be the tree laden with ornaments, a couple of children in pyjamas sitting in front of it, completely fascinated; there'll be a man's voice coming from another room and she'll whirl around in the midst of all this light, grinning from ear to ear, in a sparkling dress and worn shoes. Her own movie. Her personal mythology. Her victory over the dragons.

The decorations, carefully wrapped, have accumulated year after year. She sometimes rearranges the little pieces in their boxes to make more room. Then puts them back in the closet behind other, taller boxes so she won't have to look at them every day.

For some years now she hasn't been able to tolerate the presence of these boxes, but she still goes on buying ornaments. The game becomes superstition.

This year, she feels invested with some unfamiliar courage. An ill-timed urge to defy life and the dragons. She has turned down all the invitations she received for Christmas Eve. Above all, didn't buy any ornaments. She's alone in her apartment this Christmas night, drinking champagne, sitting on a stool in front of her mirror. With her forced smile, her sparkling dress and her worn shoes.

What she finds simple with the two of you is that she doesn't need to open her mouth to pronounce certain words distinctly so you'll be there. She just has to look deep into the mirror and you'll appear. First of all in a halo of mist, then little by little your features, your eyes, your entire faces deep in the mirror.

Tonight nothing is urgent. Nothing needs to be explained. She just has to be there on a stool, holding a drink, and everything names itself. Easily, without haste, without excess. So the world will be less hostile, so the dragons will stay cowering in their cages. Simply the image of a woman in a mirror, beautiful, with just enough heartbreak in her eyes to suggest a family resemblance with you.

When the night is over, at the hour when people go home after the party, no one notices this woman who is singing softly as she loads three boxes into the trunk of her car; no one notices her driving down to the port with all her windows rolled down; nor does anyone pay attention to this woman who is making her way on foot, with her three boxes, to the end of the dock. No one sees her solemnly throwing, one by one, some small shiny objects, each time hailing all the Christmas trees she's never decorated.

But in the morning, when people see the ornaments scattered across the ice imprisoned by the docks, they don't know if they should laugh or be alarmed. They don't know if they should see in these artifacts the cynical tokens of their young gods, outraged by the night that's just over, by laughter that was too coarse, by the unbelievable abundance of the tables, by the incurable frivolity. Or, on the contrary, a mark of approval for their attempt at amnesia.

Christmas. A day suspended, an armistice. The town sleeps and digests. A territory conquered by winter, frail light, sculptured whiteness.

Water runs in the distance, a silent image, reassuring. The hours trace furrows in the snow all the way to the river. Slowly.

Some places resound: parks where children slide, dark movie theatres, pedestrian malls. The festivities stretch out.

Later on, the summing-up. The performance isn't over yet. There are still lamps to be lit, rooms to inhabit, extra places to set at the table.

Strategies will come later. On days of courage and wind. Today: a sacred word. Its music wraps a town now free of all desire.

How to be part of the festivities? Or at any rate make people think that you are, that you aren't betraying the expectation on their faces, the amazing fervour with which they strut about laughing, wanting to be happy together?

In the background, the girl observes them. Family, perennial ivy clinging to the tree from roots to crown. Their paths branch off but one can still walk along with them side by side and, if one wants, stretch out one's arm and hold hands.

The girl studies the ritual, which is absolutely identical to that of previous years. The decorations are in the same places, the tree as well. The table is set the same way. Through this ritual, the history of the family is unwrapped and displayed, with particular attention to memory so that the party will unfold properly, so that the wounds of each member of the family, the silences, the black holes, will all be masked. Because even if it's imperfect or incomplete, at least the family has the merit of driving away the demons that mark with a red-hot iron everything that's recognizable as a sign of the future.

The idea is not to pretend but to behave as before: the excitement of a perfectly happy little girl surrounded by ribbons and torn wrapping paper; the bursts of laughter around a table where people are about to gorge themselves as at no other time all year; the fabulous aromas, abundance, surplus, excess. The unavoidable dues that the family extracts from its members for services rendered over the past twelve months.

The girl would gladly join in their enthusiasm, would like to respond to their ardour. She's touched by the warmth of the pack, by the fire they feed generously, by the tribal chant they're trying to pass on because the night is too dark, because the sky above their heads is too high, because the isolation of the stars and planets calls out to their own. Because they're no doubt obeying an age-old instinct that will make them endure, they think, beyond what ties them together.

But she is also irritated by their insistence, their profession of faith. By the way they deny the present, weigh their words so they'll be inscribed as an inheritance, so they'll help them live. What she sees is a lean pack huddled around a puny fire on a bitterly cold night. And the fundamental question is to know how to survive. Alone or as part of a group.

As for the rest, there have been no blunders. The girl has received lots of presents, which are right for her, actually. She is moved by certain gifts that seem to address her distress: music, books, reproductions of works of art. In the end, she gives in to the festivities, lets herself be filled with its sounds. Her brothers' laughter, her father's firm voice, dishes being stacked, papers crumpled. This day won't change anything, but it won't do any harm. With a little luck this day may even build some memories that will serve as moorings to which she can attach her life.

For those who know how to read signs, it's becoming obvious that the two of you are impatient to be fully returned to the town. The party's nearly over. People are starting to count the days before they go back to work or school. Visitors pay one last call on family and friends before they go home again. The town is resuming a regular, neutral rhythm. The newspapers are running ads for sales. Merchandise is being marked down. And so are feelings. Everyone's finished with wishes, with promises too hard to keep. They've dreamed under the influence of alcohol and festivities. But before the awakening is too brutal they would rather take up their everyday life again, with its tidy columns of figures and days.

You know all that. But mortals are blind in the presence of their gods. They don't know what state of mind you'll come back in to haunt the site. They hope for the calm version, the one that will let them take refuge under protective wings; they fear the terrifying version, the one marked by thunderbolts and plague.

Despite the festive air that has assuaged the town, people are not healed; they still blame themselves for not having seen you put the raft in the water, they feel responsible for every deed they were unable to do. And now that the two of you have become bigger, stronger than they are, now that your shadows hold sway over their lives, the future has become opaque to them.

She's quite happy that calm has been restored. She could get up and declare *Mission Accomplished*. As usual. But not this year. Even though everything conformed with what was expected of her and the festivities. Everyone saw her piling on efforts and fervour, of course, but this year something was broken inside, there was a leak that she plugged just long enough for the festivities and allows to flow now that they're over.

She too wondered how to be part of the festivities. She asked herself the question at the table where things were flying by on their own, at full speed, eluding her grasp. It's not that she's trying to hang on to them. She knows instinctively the destiny of families, what's happening now, and soon, and later on.

Her eyes light on a poignant girl who is silently loosening all the threads that hold her to this house, this garden, to herself. Their eyes sometimes meet. They feign ignorance of these coloured threads that are hanging down and beginning to cover the floor. But they both purse their lips in the same way, with the same concern, and it's the only sign of tenderness they share in the face of this childhood that is constantly unravelling.

And so she holds tight and plays along. Gesticulates and smiles. It's not even a desperate attempt to hang on to something that's running away. It's a kind of training, a way of being herself in the midst of those she loves with a passion. There are other ways, she knows that, but she's forgotten them, they've been lost, shipped far from the walls of this house.

She kept her word and organized the festivities as was fitting. Allowed each of them to have a childhood worthy of their expectations, a childhood to be carefully folded up in their luggage and taken away. Kept her loved ones away from scorn and close to the warmth of the lamps. And now a girl sitting at the table, with her absent expression, her nonchalant way of playing with the fork on her plate, is a brisk reminder that she must remember those other ways.

She didn't let the festivities drag out. Quickly put away the decorations, got rid of the tree. Finds herself surrounded by the usual objects and colours, those that will continue to shelter the family's little clamour.

The time has come to take inventory. She sits down one morning with a sheet of squared paper and tries to draw one up. At the top of the page she writes in big black letters, "What's left?", then divides the page into three columns, though she doesn't know why — perhaps to make it look somewhat serious or official. For a long time she searches for the correct words, the exact words. And yet those written on her list, each in its own column, strike her as incongruous, untidy. She's surprised to see listed the words *fountains, famine, slamming shutters.* Words that aren't part of her everyday vocabulary. Words that have thrown themselves forcefully onto the sheet of paper and refer to nothing except their own truth. Words no one has ever whispered to her.

She continues to fill columns, then pages. Heaps of words pile up, fill in the spaces. She doesn't understand this little game, but she perseveres. Hides her notebooks so no one can see how she's trying to glue her life back together again.

Slack days, growing longer. Breathtaking cold. The heart of winter. An exposed nerve. The town deserted. A few rare passersby hurrying, faces muffled in wool. Sky a leathery blue. Creaking of metal, cracking of trees, scraping of ice.

The price to be paid for the parties. Biting cold after Epiphany. It settles in without warning and paralyses the town. No one complains. People are even a little relieved at the numbness it brings on. Everything is reduced to the minimum. They conserve their energy for essential activities: getting from house to work, doing a quick shopping. And then, most of all, going home.

The rest is put off. The cold freezes words, hands, brains. So much so that people avoid dreaming, talking, touching one another. It's another kind of respite. And at this point people are no longer trying to think of how they should be behaving.

The cold wave doesn't affect everyone in the same way. Rather than going numb, she feels stimulated. Something like a cold shower that pulls her out of her lethargy. Now every morning, theatrically, she opens the closet door and gazes inside: the three boxes are no longer there. And that realization is enough to keep up the new, ill-defined courage she displays. Then, at her mirror, she verifies that the two of you are there, slowly runs the back of her hand over the smooth surface. Wonders how much time she has left for children, how long her body's mechanisms will allow it. Already she has reached the age of high-risk pregnancies. But her body hasn't betrayed her. Not yet. Although in this mirror, in this customary image of her fatigue, it murmurs to her to hurry up; the time for a reprieve is nearly up, her expectations of life are starting to be numbered. And because everything in this town ends up at the river, it's the image of an embryo in its accumulation of blood that she suddenly sees floating in the depths of the mirror. The image of another act of courage lost in time and space, one that, in her ignorance of the future, in the certainty of youth, she chose to send back to the sea via the town's sewers.

Some mornings weigh more heavily. Heavier the covers that have to be pulled off, the body that has to be forced into line. Sometimes at the mirror she points her finger at the two of you and utters her most hated words:

career, office, success, productivity. Reminds you that you've escaped the stupid frenzy of work. Then she loyally returns to the battalion. Puts together her public persona. Spits out the right words at the right time. Writes up technical assessments, allocates sums of money, stacks file folders on her desk. All those pointless things that wear out neurons, muscles, arteries.

Did you take pity on her, on that mortal terrorized by the looming image of her own decline? For months you have fed on her distress, on her awkward airs at the mirror. She's faithful to you. Honours her gods at both the darkest and the most luminous hours. Sends out her poor messages with no concern for what you might demand of her.

A morning like any other. The alarm goes off. She gets up. Shower, hot water on her body. A grey day, scalding coffee. Sits at her table, has breakfast. On the radio, human dramas come down to the number of cars stolen in the town in the course of the year just ended, to the probable increase in mortgage rates over the one just beginning. She is elsewhere, distracted, her mind blank, hasn't noticed that she has set three places at the table. Two empty places across from her. Yours. Your respective spaces.

First, panic. Fear that she's losing it. The taboo word: insanity. The other taboo word: loneliness. Which could make her do anything at all to fill the empty space, even the space at a little kitchen table eighty centimetres in diameter.

She hurries out of her apartment. Calms down at work. Everything is functioning normally: head, reflexes, motor responses. She hasn't fallen apart.

When she comes home that evening she switches on just one lamp, makes as little noise as possible and calmly puts away the plates and cutlery. Something inside her implores her to stop being afraid, to see instead the desire of the gods to be at her side.

The next morning, she sets three places at the table.

Winter is hanging on. The town is in a dreamlike state, a kind of coma. People have been believing in the power of time. They tell themselves over and over that you'll let go in the end, that you'll absolve the town, or else destroy its memory. And that everything will go back to the way it was before. Individuals will stop feeling that they've betrayed, that they haven't measured up. The town will begin again with young children who will be happy, who won't look over where the cliffs are, who'll never stand on the beams at the very end of the docks. People won't leave those children by themselves, they'll feed them with reassuring images, talk to them about the future as a fabulous light they must hope for, must dream about at night just before they fall asleep. Those children will be saved. And then we too will be saved. Because even though you've been raised to the rank of heroes, for months now have been treated with remarkable affection, everyone knows perfectly well that you're just two vanquished youths who slashed open the chest of this town, who left it gaping and were in no hurry to show the town how to close the wound.

They started waiting for spring the way people wait for the Messiah. It came without disorder. Brought back warmth to the air, orchestrated the breakup of the ice on the river, freed the sandbars. Made the geese come back for a break before heading north. People feel as if they can finally tie up loose ends. Go back to square one.

During the winter they fed themselves on grief that everyone made his own. Now no one's hungry any more. They've had enough. They need to turn their backs on that pain, stop taking it head-on, letting it beat against their bones till it's exhausted. Then oblivion will come. The town will go back to being one where nothing out of the ordinary happens. A town where a chastened river flows.

But no one knows how to get things moving.

Everyone's waiting for a sign. Everyone's hoping at least one of their number will rise up crying, with upraised arms and threatening fists. They would follow that person. Or else a sign of another kind: a burning bush, an apparition in a grotto, a cloud of black birds coming from the river. Then, in the presence of that sign, they would call on specialists of the soul, of the past, the future, on experts in karma of all kinds who would announce to the people that in the end their young gods had forgiven them. There would be a huge sigh of relief. It would be like the end of a flood, a famine, an earthquake. Rebuilding: that would keep them busy, that would diminish the pain. But nothing happens. Occasionally people are startled. There was that tremendous fire in a downtown hotel that claimed no victims, that left only a pile of embers. As no one knew how to read the ashes, no one could say it was a tangible sign from the young gods. There was also a landslide farther south, a few kilometres from town. The road opened up, two homes were carried away like houses of cards, but there too no one knew how to read the mud.

Yet you were starting to give them signs. Signs they didn't see, busy as they were studying the fire, the thunderbolts and the earth. Signs that were discreet but as real as the snake that takes refuge under the stones, as the bird and its song at dawn, as the key turned slowly in the lock so as not to waken anyone.

You are sincere; they're so clumsy.

They plead with you to be patient. They're on their feet but blind. They also tell you that they're not all the same. That some have a pressing need for oxygen, that certain wounds are urgent. That they can't all be saved at the same time. That they'll wait their turn. In a way, through their sincerity, they also urge you not to make the same demands as the other gods who think they've done so much for them.

As for the river, it's turning pale in the spring sunlight, while the odours of salt and seaweed come back to the town, and the anguished cries of shorebirds.

And when the town turns its head, it tells itself that perhaps it's from the blue out there that salvation will come.

PART TWO

THE DISTURBANCES OF THE RIVER

I

THE DESERT WATER

The girl got through the winter, put up with the emptiness and the cold. Lulled questions and doubts. Like everyone else. As if she'd been walking straight ahead for days and days, aimlessly, with no will or hope, and now, in the full force of this springtime, she realized that her tired footsteps had brought her to the rim of the desert. That ahead of her lay another emptiness, yet one more. That everything that made her life and took it apart was merely one form of emptiness after another.

Sometimes a surge of unbelievable anguish rises in her. To make it pass, the girl goes to walk on the docks. She sees herself again in her dream, advancing into the water, then coming to a halt. She asks herself questions. Did you two come up against the same wall, the same nothingness? Did the fact of building a raft populate the desert? Did it bring you any relief? And when you left, at the precise moment when you loosed the lines that held you to shore, what were you feeling? Were you still filled with anguish or had you left that on the shore with everything else? Were you happy? Or at least feeling good? There is never any reply except the receding river, the sound of the wind, the light that pierces everything.

The desire to know your story, the need to know, obsesses her. And it's fitting. You are there, filling great gaps in her mind, occupying the nothingness. She asks questions, waits for your answers.

As she walks along the docks, one thing becomes imperative. She has to go out on the river. She has to know.

And learn. It would be a way of coming closer to you, of getting some answers, perhaps. It would be a grandiose act. She'd buy a ticket, board the ferry, leave. Leave! Move! She repeats those words. She would question the surface of the water, the horizon, the air, the sky, she would close her eyes, would think of herself sitting on the raft between you, would pay the utmost attention to the rhythm of your breathing, would put her hand on your chests to measure the beating of your hearts. Finally, she'd penetrate your mystery. And maybe, with a little luck or good will, you would finally reveal to her whether the river is a better choice than the desert.

The day would be calm. A weekday. Fine weather, with no wind. She would make the round trip. Three full hours on the river, moving away from the world, watching the town shrink, become hazy, then a minuscule line, then this blue all around, this immeasurable quantity of air just for her. Little by little see the other world, the other shore take shape. Have the impression she's discovering America. Feeling very much a stranger, and actually being one, for once. Then repeat the crossing in the opposite direction, watch things come back to her, return to the town with another way of seeing, suffused with grace from having almost touched you.

She doesn't want to talk about it. Knows there's nothing exceptional about her plan. She'd just be doing what they call "the tourist crossing." Couldn't bear being asked why she'd done it. And in any event, she never volunteers anything. She'd go away one morning and come back that afternoon. Should she need a pretext, anything would do. Something tells her that it would be a day like the day of the two trees when she was a child, that a key would be given to her. A secret. A rendezvous. Some place other than the desert.

She has set a date, choosing one just far enough away to nurture her plan. Has started a journal of the crossing, as she calls it, carefully noting everything she ought to notice to jog her memory once she's back, to show her what road to take afterwards.

The girl has been drawn into the game of preparations, checking out travel articles in the stores. Has bought a raincoat that folds up into a tiny package, a Swiss Army knife and a pair of sneakers.

Her pallor is gone. People think she's not so sad. There's a spring in her step, she holds her head higher. She listens to old Beatles songs at night, cooped up in her room.

To ease her impatience, she sometimes spreads out on her bed the things she'll take with her. She's made a list of what she'll need for eating. Checks to see if it will all fit in her backpack. Repeats the exercise. It's not enough, the backpack is still half empty. Going away with half one's baggage is like half going away. It's ridiculous, amateurish. It's like not going away at all. She goes back to her desert, to the dream in which she has her feet in the mud and doesn't make any progress.

It's not enough. It has to be a real journey. With a real duration. To lose all notion of time, not know the hour or the date. To be able to tell herself that she won't come home that evening or the next. To allow herself time to wait for the real answers, for the real images to come to the surface.

She'd leave, buy a one-way ticket. And after that, she'd see. The river isn't there just to be crossed, you can follow it too. Upstream or downstream. Towards the solitude of the gulf or towards another town, much bigger than this one, with other cafés, other docks, other ghosts.

The preparations have to be reconsidered. It would be easy to fill the empty part of her backpack. But to leave for more than a day she'd pretty well have to disclose the fact of the journey. And then would come the predictable reaction of the woman with the squirrels and the orange juice. A spoilsport. This journey belongs to her. She'll have to lie. How can she explain something she doesn't understand herself? How can she explain the plea from those faces that for months have been displayed on the refrigerator door? How can she explain the desert, the paralysed muscles, the disturbing murmur of the world behind café windows? How can she confess that nothing can induce the slightest desire, the slightest enthusiasm? That she can't stir up any fire in herself? That she is already without a voice? That she avoids looking at her reflection in store windows for fear of seeing a stooped woman with white hair? She wants to go in search of something new, unknown. Seek truths of the kind offered by tarot cards or tea leaves.

By way of an answer she'd get arguments, warnings. Protective instincts wanting to enfold her, hold onto her. And then the utter defeat in her mother's eyes. The girl would let her talk, then leave anyway. It could happen that way, but there was a risk. With other people, you never know. Their fears and doubts pierce your skin and sometimes insinuate themselves so deeply that you accept them inside yourself, as if they'd always been there. For the time being, a girl is going resolutely off to meet a raft; if she stops along the way and turns around, she wants it to be her own distress that dictates it, and no one else's.

To the words *move* and *leave*, which she writes at the top of every page in her travel diary, is added one that she greets at first with bewilderment. It has come to sit alongside the other two, without her being fully aware of it. She didn't know immediately what it was trying to tell her. She writes it across the page again and again, tries various styles of penmanship, then starts a new page, places it alone, upright, in the middle. Pulls back a little, not knowing if what she's just discovered on this nearly blank page should leave her frightened or overjoyed. A temptation, a genuine desire: *disappear*. To leave a letter saying, Don't worry. That she's gone on a journey, that she needs a change of air, needs to be alone. Facile turns of phrase, practically formulas. As far as her mother was concerned, she'd be insistent. Would weigh her words, sound reassuring, promise to phone. Her letter would buy peace, with no room for discussion.

Keep both her itinerary and her departure day secret. Wait till the time is right before leaving the house, drop the letter on the kitchen table. Go down to the docks. Wait a while. Board a ferry, near where you put your raft in the water. Once on the boat, forget the date of her birth, the ordinary town on the bank of this vast river. Forget all those who gravitate around her. *Disappear*. To be an insubstantial body without memory or desire, one that flares briefly, then vanishes. To let her gaze light on the horizon. Let the little voice rise within her.

This is starting to seem like a dream.

The girl has written dozens of letters. There's always something essential missing. The message is either flat or too explicit. She tries to adopt a solemn tone with just enough distance to inspire respect. Doesn't want others to think it's a whim. Nor does she want the words to sound spiteful; she has no scores to settle with those who will read the letter.

It happens one morning at five o'clock. Her departure is like one of the Beatles songs she listens to in her room at night. She goes downstairs in absolute silence, places the letter on the kitchen table, trembling. The room is already flooded with light. It's a beautiful day, with no wind. It will be the way she hoped it would be.

Before she leaves, she walks around the kitchen as if for the last time and wonders if it's possible to erase things, to live without all these details that make up life. She feels uncomfortable in this place that in a few seconds will be quite simply transferred into her memory. The girl does one last thing before she leaves. Her sole act of cruelty. She takes your photo off the door of the fridge, where it continues to resist time and tempers. She knows that it doesn't belong to her. That she's stealing it from someone who in two hours will turn to it instinctively and question it.

The two of you watch the scene. First the fullness of the world: the dawn light streaked with shadow. The prodigious odours, the rustling of leaves, the bustling of birds now at feeding time. The customary silence of the town just before waking. And the great breath of the river down below. Then a minuscule dot. A petite girl walking with her luggage on her back, her new sneakers on her feet and your crumpled, yellowing photo between two pages of her diary.

As if she'd had a first answer.

When she arrives at the docks, her first instinct is to look at the time. Her letter hasn't been read yet. She's surprised by the activity in the port. The flurry around her shows her what life can contain: fishermen, businessmen, tourists. Others have got up before her, then, have already cast their eyes on the flames of this day. She thinks that there are no more Americas to be discovered, that every centimetre of this planet has been touched, trampled; insects, birds, plants have all been catalogued. Everything she'll learn on this journey can be found in books. But which ones, exactly?

She is the first person to board the ferry. Nervously checks the time. Perhaps at this very moment eyes are scanning the letter. Anxiously she turns to look at the docks, as if it were possible that she'd been spotted and that someone had come to get her. Also keeps checking to see if there's a familiar face among the passengers. It isn't easy to disappear.

Just before the engines are started, before the boat begins to vibrate, there's a moment of unexpected silence, a state of grace lasting just a few seconds, long enough for the girl to feel her lungs being smoothed out upon contact with the sea air, to feel each of her muscles relaxing too.

A boat leaves the port of a little town, moving slowly away from the dock. A common, everyday event. A girl on the foredeck resembles a figurehead.

Shortly after departure she has a silly hunch that the crossing won't unfold according to the images that have settled into her head. She wishes it could be like church. With something sacred, contemplative about it. She could almost kneel down, her body leaning slightly towards the water that foams as it races towards the back of the boat. She sees herself invoking you in an incantation you couldn't resist. But in this boat that becomes like a nutshell as it moves away, she can find no privacy. The agitation on the docks goes on. Loudspeakers crackle with easy-listening music that's devastating. The luminous beauty of the morning, its mildness, has united all the travellers — more numerous than usual — on the deck, though generally they stay inside where they can sit and drink coffee. To the rumbling of the boat, to the sound of the music, are added the passengers' conversations. Excited tourists talk about the whales they hope to spot, workers talk about fishing quotas, the government, the cod now taking refuge in the muscles of grey seals — which have to be slaughtered, and soon. About the forests, too, that are being clear-cut. About unemployment, which eats away at hope.

The town has followed her onto the boat.

All the water in the river rushes into her lungs at once; this won't be her journey. She won't inhabit this place, she'll remain an outsider on this deck as she is everywhere else. The world doesn't call to her, won't merge with her. Sky, river, air have joined forces to make her understand that everything is to be shared. That there are a good hundred others like her on the deck this morning, cutting the sky into pieces, breathing the same sea spray, their eyes focusing on the same furious blue; each of them tries to fill the void by talking loudly, by clutching at his neighbour's sleeve. Here too.

The girl leaves the foredeck and goes to the stern, where it's calmer. She's finally here, on the river. That's what matters. Maybe it's even trying to reveal its secrets to her. Its texture is changing. Great shuddering areas replace the mirrors, separated by lines of foam. One can make out the currents. The colour changes constantly. It's not the tremendous, uniform mass one sees from shore, but a sort of mosaic, and seen up close it loses its power. All its fragility is revealed. This isn't the answer she's been expecting. Her journey is over. She's convinced of that. Everything rings false. Like her, the world has no voice. The girl feels ridiculous with her backpack. She takes her diary from one of her pockets, pulls out your photo and throws the diary in the water. Since there won't be a journey, there won't be any words. As for the photo, she hesitates. You did exist. You did achieve a raft, a letter. You did find a response. But you won't come back to the surface, close to her face leaning out over the water, you'll remain silent. It's not your fault, you can't do anything for her or anyone else. She has put together this false journey for herself the way you put together the raft. She has dreamed. And now that she's here, nothing has changed: the murmur of the town fills the foredeck and the river is merely a variation of the desert.

She stays there with her head leaning out over the water. Doesn't see the other shore approaching. A woman comes up to her, touches the girl's arm and asks if she's feeling sick, if she's all right. Even when she makes herself as small as possible, when every cell in her body calls out for silence and obliteration, the mob reappears with its peculiar, discreet compassion.

The boat docks. The deck empties, people go to their cars. The tourists didn't see any whales. For those who are making the round trip without disembarking, a voice sputters in the loudspeakers that the boat will leave again in thirty minutes. There's also a reminder of the schedule for that day's crossings.

The girl has no choice now but to get off. She feels as if she's arriving nowhere. This place has no soul. There's just one pier, the extension of a narrow road that goes down to the river. Cars are lined up waiting for the next departure. There's no harbour or marina. You have to climb to the other road that leads to the village.

She is the only one who walks onto the road. A car slows down, stops near her. Somebody offers her a lift. She shakes her head no. She'll walk. Even if there's no longer a journey, no diary, her body, her muscles are working. She's no longer motionless, captive, inside her dream. She is moving. She goes up the hill in one burst, anxious to leave this ridiculous place, this rutted asphalt road that runs into the river. Her pack is already starting to feel heavy on her back. At the top of the hill she heads for the village. Walks for a long time. The sun is beating down. Roadside landscape. Gravel under her feet. The demented noise of trucks in her ears.

It's not yet noon. Her feet hurt because of the new sneakers. If she were to be granted one wish, only one, if she should suddenly meet a genie from a lamp, she would wish that New York would appear at the next turn in the road, or Paris, or Hong Kong, that she would find herself in the world's abundance instead of in its destitution.

You are far away at this moment, buried, creased, deep in her pocket. She occupies the space. Suffers the laws of physics, which tire her back, scrape her feet.

She throws away the contents of her backpack. Keeps only the food and what she needs to eat it. Seeing her clothes in the ditch, she imagines herself dying in that hole, in that bed of damp earth safe from other people's eyes. Noisy trucks and cars wouldn't assault her, they would lull her and she'd soon close her eyes on this useless sky. She wouldn't be found for a while. Because of the summer heat, insects, animals, her body would decompose quickly. Only her clothes wouldn't deteriorate.

And one fine morning a truck driver would stop on the roadside to take a leak and he'd discover the scattered clothing. The pile of bones, protected by the grass, mud and gravel, wouldn't be apparent.

She gets back on the road. Feels light. She has just died in a ditch yet she goes on walking. At the limit of her vision the road turns and gives the impression that it's descending towards the river again. Perhaps it's New York or Hong Kong. Or the paradise of little girls who've died in ditches.

The village appears. A logical outgrowth of the landscape that has accompanied the girl all morning. Nestled deep in a cove, it stretches alongside the road, which follows the river. In fact, it's not the village that stands out but the road, which doesn't even run through town but goes along one side, leaving it alone and destitute, then climbs again once it's past the village. It's a place where people don't linger, they pass by.

She's not surprised. Things persist in betraying her. And to forget that she's not in the place where she should be, the girl continues to put one foot down and then the other. She arrives at the village to the sound of the noon bells. The heat is oppressive. The air doesn't circulate. The tide is low, the odours of seaweed and sewer mingle, grip the place. She's hungry, tired. At this time of day the village appears to be sleeping. The girl goes down to the beach to eat. She sits on the rocks. Her feet hurt. She takes bread and cheese from her bag. The Swiss Army knife too. She thinks that there are few objects as remarkable as this knife. At school, when she was a child, she was sometimes given an exercise that she took to be a game. She was supposed to draw on a sheet of paper everything precious, all the beings, things, situations she was fond of. In other words, what keeps people alive. And on another sheet, everything that she rejected, refused without compromise. Today, the first object she'd draw would be this knife. A piece of the world you can

hold in your hand, a useful, solid object that has survived over time, ever since the day when some living
being, hungry and angry, tore open the body of an animal with the sharp side of a stone he'd just picked up on
the shore of a river like this one. She cuts bread and
cheese, feels connected for a moment to that hunger.

What would she add to the list, after the knife? Are
there moments in one's life when you must cover blank
sheets of paper with drawings? Must you place them in
front of yourself and select the page that will decide what
happens next? What she'd like is to be able to name spontaneously, in order, what she would draw if she were to
repeat the exercise. In her mind, though, the pages remain blank, except for the drawing of the Swiss Army
knife in one corner at the top.

The girl looks at the river. Precisely across from her,
on the other side, a town is breathing amid the harsh
whiteness of the light. The harsh whiteness of the letter
that a woman has been reading again and again all morning. The harsh whiteness of classroom walls, with an
empty seat in the last row. The damp whiteness of the
pages of a diary upon the water of the river. The girl
finally falls asleep, leaning against the rocks, safe from
other people's eyes, facing a nameless cove, facing the
river she's just crossed but not in triumph. Alone, huddled up, she slips into a sleep as heavy as the air around
her.

The light has changed. The river has come closer to
her. The girl wakes with a start. Like a hunted animal. In
the same way that, at this same time somewhere else in
the madness of the world, people are waking to the sound
of mortar fire. For a moment she doesn't know the *where*,
the *when*, the *how*, the *why*. The noise of trucks and the
pain of her blistered feet bring her back to reality. It's
hot. Her hair is sticking to her forehead, the nape of her
neck. The girl is thirsty, the water she brought isn't cool
now. She goes back to the village, her feet hurting. She

walks along the streets for a while. Sees women with baby carriages, old people sitting on dilapidated galleries. She goes into a grocery store to buy water. People stare at her. Young men accost her, their gazes sullen, their voices impoverished.

It's starting to feel like the beginning of a nightmare. She has fallen into a trap. Here the world reveals itself in all its pettiness. She becomes aware that there's more than one way to be an outsider. Not just the way she's always known, where one passes through things without touching them, staying off to one side, never raising one's voice — the way that uproots gently, painlessly — but the other way too, the one practised here, the one that questions, that doesn't recognize the river any more, that tears away the skin, that wounds without killing.

A single certainty: in this entire story one person hasn't betrayed her. One person calls her back with an understanding voice, one person can bring her peace. She will go back to the river. A van drops her off at the top of the hill that leads to the ferry. It wasn't her choice. Outside a garage she met an elderly man who was about to get back on the road. When he saw the girl with her backpack it seemed obvious to him that she was going to take the six-thirty boat. He simply offered to drop her off there. He spoke to her with a natural human kindness that surprised her. He was travelling by himself in this van he'd transformed into a place to live in. Summers up north, winters down south. He had blue eyes. The girl has seated herself behind him. Her feet and her back don't hurt now. She smiles as she looks at the road she travelled in the opposite direction this morning.

Is it possible that he was saving her? He didn't talk much, didn't ask any questions, dropped her off where he'd said he would. She didn't have to make any decisions. He just showed up and took her away from that hostile place. They wish one another good luck. The girl is back by the side of the road.

On the boat, the atmosphere is different now. The passengers move slowly, not frantically. A sort of lassitude circulates from one to another. Voices are slower too. The loudspeakers are silent. The end of the day imposes its own law, its rhythm. Imposes in particular a remarkable splendour because of the light, which is at once gentle and violent, and the river's unbelievable calm at this time of day, and the fatigue that forces the passengers to be quiet. The girl feels she's in the right place. Will she get a second chance, a second rendezvous with this river? She would let herself be carried away, would insist on nothing. So much the better if, into the bargain, the river whispered some answers anyway. She is sitting cross-legged, has pulled off her shoes. Blisters mark both feet symmetrically, in the same places. She knows instinctively that this crossing will be better than the one this morning. The world's bitterness is erased along with the daylight. The light, the odours call for reconciliation. It's not yet peace, not even some kind of well-being. Just a fleeting impression of being at one with everything that surrounds her, of entering that splendour, of touching each of its components until she becomes that light, that current, that mass of white metal, those voices, those eyes. She almost wants to believe that the journey is beginning.

She is filled with contradictory feelings. In her throat, a bitter taste refuses to dissolve. She's ashamed. Wasn't able to go any farther, stupidly lost the journey the way one loses one's keys, one's notebooks. Ashamed of having sore feet after wanting movement so badly. The girl sees her dream again and wonders if she's inventing the outcome: after advancing in the water up to her waist, after her trembling and her inability to move, here she is, simply, pathetically going back to the shore. What strength did she lack? What audacity did she not have? By sabotaging this journey has she sabotaged all the others that will come after it? This is the only momentum that's come to her. A flash in the pan. Wings that fall limp as soon as they're spread.

Shortly after departure, most of the passengers on deck go inside. From where she's sitting the girl feels as if she's close to the water, as if she could brush it with her fingers without having to lean over. As if the river were now coming to her. The girl has never faced death from so close. She'd just have to step over the guardrail and let herself fall. A flash. It would happen so fast there wouldn't be time for anyone to come running. At first people would be transfixed; then, when they were able to cry out, when the boat finally slowed down, the water in her lungs would already have snuffed out whatever fire was left in her.

The future doesn't exist, she thinks, because it can assume multiple faces. Which are necessarily false. Sometimes, perhaps, one of those faces will finally become incarnate. And then it can be named. But already it's no longer the future. Since morning, several faces have followed one another: that of a girl walking, that of a girl at the bottom of a ditch or under the river water, also that of a girl sitting behind an old man in a small van.

Blinded by the setting sun, she's beginning to think the future can be anything at all — anything except this lack of fire, of vitality that takes up all the space in her head.

Nothing lasts. The boat sails on, the light slants. The spell will pass. Nothing will remain of this beauty that heals as much as it tears apart. Soon the river will no longer reveal itself in its final nakedness, the light in its waning fervour. Confederates. The allies of a girl heading home, heading back to her usual desert. As the boat approaches, a group of eider ducks takes flight; they line up behind one another like living arrows, and the colour of the setting sun makes them appear to be on fire. The girl watches them, sees them break free of the river, the landscape, and she tells herself that others have found a way to travel the world, to inhabit only its brilliance.

A small group of young people arrives on deck, boys and girls a little older than she is; they speak loudly, with a European accent. Cameras around their necks, road maps in hand. An organized trip. They laugh, exult when a seal's head emerges from the water. Now and then they look in her direction. They're wearing clothes in garish shades, many colours. They're beautiful, unique. She pretends she doesn't see them but she studies their every move, the way they lean on the guardrail, the warmth of their voices, the fire in their eyes. They seem terribly at ease here, they form a universe, compact but open, self-sufficient. The light, the river offer themselves to them without reservation.

A little farther away, a woman tries to hold back a very young child who's carried away by the excitement of his first steps. The child dashes towards the middle of the deck, laughing. He lets out shrill little cries, alone, triumphant at the centre of the world. The attention of all the passengers is directed to the child. One of the young men walks over to him, joining in his play, taking the child by one hand and lifting him up to his shoulders. The child laughs even harder. The others applaud.

The girl has followed the scene with the others. And to hide her discomfort at this time when everyone should be feeling like brothers, so the others don't make out the desert on her face, she starts rummaging frantically in her backpack. Takes out the rest of the bread and cheese, the Swiss Army knife.

She isn't hungry. But at least if people look at her they'll realize she's not just a motionless shadow sitting on the bench. She doesn't want to attract attention. Simply wants to be erased from this scene, wants no one to spot this dull girl on the edge of their brightness. She cuts bread, cheese, feigning diligence. Takes her time because when she's finished she won't know what to do with her hands, will be forced to look up, and then the others may think she wants to join them. The girl twirls her knife, plays with the shimmering light. Every detail becomes infinitely large. She looks up abruptly. This is what you have to know about the world: this boat like an ark, the identical light on the river and on the knife blade, a girl on the fringe, men, women, children, young people in the roundness of things. The grace of gestures and faces. Life, too vast for her own hands.

What must she do? How can she overturn the order of the world? She could get up and walk over to the group of young people. Ask for binoculars. And would that perhaps be enough to usher her into an easy life? Their smiling faces would turn towards her. Something definitive would rise in her veins. An unknown force. A push towards the top. Her heart would beat more powerfully, would resonate in her temples. Her hands would touch the cold metal of the guardrail. The wind would come up, would whip her body to the verge of pain. Someone would put his hands on her shoulders. She would be part of the trip. It won't happen.

The girl feels stupid with her carefully cut bread and cheese spread across her backpack, which she's using as a table. She finally brings the smallest piece to her lips, to give some sense to her production. It rolls around in her mouth. She wonders how long one can live without being hungry.

She keeps her eyes glued to this universe she's just assembled: the bread, the crumbs, the cheese. This territory belongs to her, will be useless to her. She has arranged the knife in the middle of the picture. Would like to take a photo: this landscape seems to her the truest one of the entire journey. To the picture she adds her own open hands on either side of the backpack. The small vein that winds across her wrist is the same colour as the river. That makes her smile. She bends her head down farther so they won't notice. Is there a second river?

Another boat with another girl on board? A river going nowhere that constantly follows the same course, doubling back on itself again and again, circulating inside the same walls? Day after day. To the point of erosion. To the point of drought.

With the tip of her knife she starts gently scratching at the little blue river. From wrist to palm, then from palm to wrist. Round trip. Makes it disappear under a trail of little white flakes of skin. The world seen from above, the river hidden by the Milky Way. The farthest destination of the journey.

Soon it will be night. The crossing is almost over. The smells have changed. The people too. They've resumed their useful, tidy motions. Have moved their luggage close to them. Put cameras back in their cases. They're tying shoelaces, buckling bags.

The girl stands up. Looks at the river behind her. It hasn't spoken, hasn't admitted anything. Not in one direction or the other. It's this boat that has raised its voice, against all expectation. The girl wishes she could convince herself that things never arrive from where we think they will. Nothing has changed since this morning. This day hasn't been the first day of Year 1. This day is dying without violence, like all the others before it. In a few minutes the boat will bump the dock, will make a jolt. Negligible.

The girl catches sight of the town spreading before her, seeming to mock her and welcome her at the same time. It's right here, in this fragile night, that she will be most lost.

The two of you are waiting for her on the dock.

She walks slowly onto the gangway, anonymous among the other passengers. A child in its mother's arms is whimpering. The loudspeakers thank the travellers in a lifeless voice and announce the schedule for tomorrow's crossings. The sun has disappeared. And that's it for today. The town is turning blue. One by one, lights punctuate the space.

When the girl steps onto the dock, she stops short, understands. People walk past her, go to their cars, to buses. They're not concerned about her. You are there. You've let her make the journey on her own. She looked for you, waited for you. You didn't come. And now she's coming back to you at the end of this day, the end of this stillborn journey, her eyes even paler, emptier, her lips dry, bitten by the sun and the sea air. She doesn't know whether to laugh or cry. Whether to show rage or joy. You are there, with your answers that can't get past your lips, with your certainties and your doubts. Which are hers as well. You've come back to wrap her in your obsessions, in your morbid affection. She puts her hand in her pocket, touches your photo. You abandoned her, returned her to herself so she could discover her own truth, so she could stop clinging to your mystery, but she's discovered nothing. Then you take her back under cover of night, in the very same place where you let go of her hand. And as the girl has no might or weapon, she'll show neither rage nor joy. She won't struggle. Won't even turn around when you shift your shadow onto hers. You bring her back to reality: she has returned. In one stroke the universe is familiar again. By looking around her, at the docks, the buildings, the boulevard that runs along the river, the girl finds herself again. At the same time, though, she has the impression that years have gone by since her departure.

Now it's a question of knowing what to do.

Night has fallen all at once. A light wind, warm and humid, has come up. The docks are empty. You won't help her turn into a pillar of salt. The best you can do is rekindle some spark in her leg muscles so she can at least loosen the knots holding her down.

Her first move: to go to the little snack bar in the marina. She organizes every one of her body's actions: walk up to the door, push it open, go inside, sit down, order a lemonade. Before her appear the house, the letter, her family — especially her mother. The blue bedroom with her absence inside. The old teddy bear left behind on the bed. In her ears, a Beatles song. Everything comes back to her at once. Her heart is pounding. She sees herself on the road home, coming to the corner of the street in front of the two big trees that wouldn't say anything. She'd go inside. Her mother would be sitting at the table. She'd be pale, her eyes red and swollen, she'd be holding the letter. She'd be surprised, would jump up, heave a sigh of relief. Of anger too, perhaps. She'd ask for an explanation. Wouldn't try to understand why she'd run away but rather the fact that she hadn't. Would interrogate her. Would try to relate the words in the letter to the presence of her daughter rooted there on the threshold.

It would be grotesque. At first her mother would think it was a kind of perversity. She'd accuse the girl of wanting to frighten her, of fabricating the journey just so she could see her devastated in her kitchen, to get revenge, to punish her — her own mother — for the loss of childhood, for everything that was unable to take shape, to settle in the girl's body, in her mind. Running away would become a personal attack on her. She would counterattack. The girl would let her talk, gesticulate. Wouldn't reply. She would observe. That story wouldn't belong to her. Let this woman facing her, making a spectacle of herself in her distress mixed with anger, be however moving; the girl would not be affected.

What would hurt, deep down in her chest, would be to stand there on the doorstep, to be back in her life among all the things and beings who knew her by name. To be there with the truth of the journey inscribed on her forehead: she couldn't do it; she'd lacked drive; no curiosity had urged her on. She wouldn't need to confess; everyone would guess. An unkept promise. A first humiliation. Shame that would settle in for good.

Imagining that she'd then have to walk across the
kitchen, go back upstairs to her room, strikes her as even
more complicated, more difficult than the day she's just
lived through. Worse yet, how is she to get up the next
morning? In the desert, every morning, every action is
the same, only serving to confirm the extent of the void
around her.

If by chance the future does exist, she has no part in
it.

The waitress comes to tell her that on weeknights
the restaurant closes early. The girl starts moving again.
Goes back to the docks instead of into town. Walks for a
while. The river is black.

The two of you are still behind her.

In her mind, things cease to exist. She's neither cold
nor afraid. Her body doesn't hurt any more. She is heading into the night, it's like her dream, the difference being that nothing holds her to the ground. Nor does anything call her. Neither siren song nor raft.

She stops at the end of the last dock, in the disused
section of the port, where no boats tie up and one sees
only rats that have found refuge in the rusty warehouses.
The ground is strewn with debris. The girl walks to the
very edge of the dock. On one side, the town: port, boats,
lighthouse. Higher up, the faint murmur of people preparing for sleep, getting into bed, closing their eyes and
hoping they won't become anxious too soon. On the other
side, the space is swallowed up by the night, by the sound
of water striking the dock, the air.

She stands utterly motionless. Images start spinning
in her head. Voices rise. The blue-eyed man with the van
tells her nicely that one can live for a hundred years and
not be saved, that the mistake is to settle into that kind
of expectation. That one can survive anything. Scarcity
as well as abundance. The cries of the child hoisted by
the young man rise too, contradicting the old man: as
soon as we're born, we await only those arms to make

us feel alive. All our lives we hope to be lifted up higher than someone else's shoulders.

The girl takes your photo from her pocket. Speaks your names as she smooths it. On the tired newsprint your two faces look like the faces of old people. She holds her arm out slowly above the water, opens her fingers. Surely you can die a second time, since you're capable of doing anything. The photo takes on the colour of the water. Perhaps it's that simple after all. Just one small motion, with no violence. One small final act of tenderness for oneself.

Then it's the turn of the Swiss Army knife. She opens the little blades into a fan. New. Unused. They stab the water with a muffled sound.

The girl is improvising. Each of her movements echoes in every fibre of her muscles. Each movement calls forth another that she hasn't foreseen. Her brain jettisons ballast, submits to the law of the body that commands everything. Then she throws in her backpack. After that she bends down, slowly unties her shoes. Straightens up and uses the metal edge of the dock to pull them off. The shoes strike the wall as they drop.

A girl at the very edge of a dock.

Her bare feet on the cold, damp metal. The small wounds from her journey start hurting again, persist in declaring their resistance. The beating of a heart concealed in each of her blisters. The final obstacles go into the water. Her belt, her denim jacket.

On the river, the glints of the harbour lights stretch out to sea as if to show the direction. On the dock, the wind strikes the sheet-metal roofs of the ruined buildings.

The girl doesn't move. Will not move. Will stand there till she's exhausted. Till her muscles let go. Till her body topples. She thinks about the Little Prince. Hopes it will be like the snake's bite. *Only a yellow flash near the ankle. Would stay there motionless for a moment. Would not cry out. Would fall slowly, the way a tree falls. It wouldn't make even a sound.*

But there too, she thinks to herself, nothing's certain. Not till the body topples. Falls like a tree. But which way? There's as much chance that she'd fall on the cement, the metal and the wood — the ground beneath her feet — as slip down past the dock and into the wet night of the river. Perhaps at the very last second a nerve, a tendon will deflect the body's trajectory. Or else, out of the blue, the brain will gain the advantage. Impose movement on the body. Perhaps she'll soar upwards like a shorebird, awkwardly, with wings that are too broad, a neck that's too long, or she'll step backwards, crying.

The two of you stand back, leaning against the wall of a warehouse.

You don't look like Wim Wenders's angels. Nor are you carrying a revolver with your finger on the trigger, as in the American movies that nourished you to the point of nausea. You observe this girl standing erect, motionless, with a little wind in her hair, just enough to make the scene more touching. You look at her, holding your breath. For the first time you're experiencing the greatest power of the gods: their silence.

II

TROUBLED WATERS

"Nobody's ever kissed me like you."
"Nobody's ever kissed me like you."
"Nobody's ever kissed me like you."
Girls in the arms of boys pronounce these words between sips of Coke. When she sees that commercial on TV she understands how attacks, wars, violence of all kinds can arise from some obscure fold in the human brain.

Spring is bursting out, with its heat, its odours, its calls for abandon, its unique way of whetting the appetite. You think she looks paler, more tired. You've learned a lot about her these past months. She hasn't stopped confiding in her mirror. It's a little as if you'd been her sons. She still sets three places at breakfast now and then. Especially on those mornings when she tries in vain to conceal the circles under her puffy eyes. The two of you are preparing for your departure. You've decided to disappear, to leave the clear water of her mirror. One morning she'd wake up and wouldn't see you. It would be over. Returned to herself, a whim of the gods. You don't want to see her sad, don't wish her any harm. You just want her to direct her calls for help to someone else. Someone who'd rush from his hiding place at the sound of her cries, who'd move from the darkness to the light, who'd look blindly for the source of her laments in the confusion of the world.

One morning at her mirror she realizes that you're no longer there. She's neither disappointed nor glad. It's

like everything else. Things come and go. Nothing at-
taches itself to her life. She opens the french door, steps
onto the balcony. The breath of the river reaches her. She's
holding on. Keeping a tight rein on her despair. She tells
herself that, in this country, at least the seasons force you
to don other odours, to inject another light into your
veins.

Sometimes she takes to her heels and goes back to
the mob downtown. Sunday morning, for instance. When
Saturday evening has been too empty, the night too bar-
ren. A café opened late that winter, near the port: The
Raft of the Medusa. People reacted badly to the name.
They saw it as an allusion. The word *raft* written in red
on the window seemed offensive. She likes going there.
Likes the audacity.

In cafés on Sunday mornings the human race bares
its secrets, offers itself freely. The people having breakfast exert a powerful fascination over her. She can recon-
struct their night from the way they bow their heads,
from what they say or don't say, from the way they scan
the newspaper or hold a cup or fork. And when the same
people come back week after week, their entire life is
unblushingly revealed. They all feel related in a way,
these lone individuals or couples sitting quietly in the
restaurant booths, their faces multiplied by the mirrors.

Some Sundays, the café is noisy. Voices carry. As if
they all had something to say, to reveal. As if it were becoming imperative to name what they see, what they
touch. Those mornings cause her more pain. Most of the
time, the atmosphere in the café is quiet. A few people
speak in low voices, display under their eyes the circles
left there by the night. Some couples stare at one another,
utter words through pinched lips, words they launch like
missiles or bottles into the sea. Other couples don't talk.
Some no longer need words, have told each other everything long ago, guess what the other has to say, plunge
into their silence together. Others, more numerous, have

exhausted everything, have seen the walls of silence going up between them. Their movements are slow, their gazes empty. They always sit near the windows in the hope of being snatched up by the world.

And then there are the loners. Some spend hours over a book, drinking cup after cup of coffee. They act as if they aren't expecting anything, aren't looking for anything. But when they raise their heads and look around, it's as if they're begging on their knees in the middle of the place, crying: "I'm here! I'm here!" And since the café isn't all that big, their cries make the walls shake, make the glasses suspended above the counter clink. No one seems to hear them.

There's another category of loners who have a totally different way of doing things. They appear fiercely attentive to what's going on in the café, but at the same time their manner is detached. There's nearly always a newspaper on their table, they take pleasure in what they're eating, don't spend hours and, at the door, exchange a few words with the waiter, laughing.

She thinks she's in a separate category. Doesn't recognize herself in either the first scenario, the Greek tragedy, or the quiet one. She has the impression she's in the too-soon-too-late category. One that's insipid, colourless, tasteless. Unique of its kind.

One Sunday morning the two of you seat a man at the table facing hers. A man who hasn't come bursting out of his lair, who hasn't been blinded, who doesn't hear cries. He doesn't belong to this town, that's perfectly obvious. She couldn't say why. He's reading the paper. At another time the sight of this man would have driven her to the barricades. Today, though, at this precise moment, in this café, in this town, on the bank of this river, he's merely one piece of reality, one more, like the other customers around her, like the irresistible aroma of hot coffee.

He is absorbed in the newspaper. She pretends she's

not watching him. Calculates how long it's been since someone important has shown up in her life. Counts the nights, the number of men to whom she's opened her door by default. Not for long. Of those who told her with a desperate look that they'd met too late but they wouldn't relinquish anything of the life they lived away from her. Also counts the number of days of crisis, of ice, of spring breakup. She panics; that's a lot of numbers.

He takes a last sip of coffee, folds up his paper, sticks it in his jacket pocket. He gets up, looks at her. No dove takes flight, no sweet perfume wafts its fragrance, no music enfolds them. He speaks to the waiter for a moment and pays his bill. He goes out. Walks past the restaurant windows. Disappears.

When she in turn leaves the café, she stands motionless for a few moments, her eyes turned to the river. She begs you softly — as if she's guessed everything — not to make her suffer any more.

The following Sunday she goes back to The Raft of the Medusa. She's known all week that she would. Doesn't really know why. Hasn't fallen in love with the man across from her, doesn't harbour any expectation, doesn't have the feeling that something is beginning, doesn't expect any miracle.

Inside the café there's an unusual feverishness. When she goes inside it takes a while for her to notice the customers' eyes all focused on the same target; some are actually standing and facing the wall where all the gazes converge. She makes her way to the table where she always sits, doesn't look at anyone. Unties her scarf, takes off her jacket, nonchalantly drapes them over the back of the chair and sits down, takes from her bag the magazine she's brought — in a word, tries to suggest to all mankind that she's a Category II loner, though she's never felt such a strong sense of solidarity with Category I.

The clients who've been standing scatter. Space opens

up in front of her. The owner of the café has just hung a painting on the stone wall, a very large painting commissioned from a young local artist. The painting, which has the same name as the café that houses it, depicts two young men on their knees, coats unbuttoned, on a tiny raft in a storm. They're supporting each other. The same pale expression, the same strands of hair stuck to their foreheads and temples. The image in the mirror, in this café. Without her inside it.

She lets out a little moan, like a bird's. The two of you have left her and come here to join her. You've come to display your anguish to the whole town. And hers as well. She shudders. Feels as if all the customers are looking at her, as if they know. The waiter sets a bowl of café au lait in front of her. She gulps half of it as if it were strong liquor.

He ambles into the café. The newspaper under his arm. Stops briefly to observe the scene: customers are arguing, calling out to one another, some are fiercely protesting the painting because the tragedy has to be forgotten, because that event mustn't become a trademark, because there are actually people in this town who could look at this painting and pronounce the words *son*, *friend*, *pupil*. Others, in contrast, talk about the collective unconscious, about memory, artistic freedom, the soul of this town.

He sits down near her, at an angle. He could almost touch her. The discussion heats up. He smiles discreetly, arms crossed, hasn't opened his paper.

She tells herself he probably doesn't understand a thing about this circus because he's undoubtedly an outsider. The young men in the painting stare at him. The urge to stand up and howl at death, like a dog. She's pale, hot, she starts to tremble.

She gets up, quickly pulls on her jacket. Thinks she's inventing a new category of loners: those who don't go to cafés, who walk the edges of precipices without paying attention, who skid at a turn in the road.

Outside, she bursts into tears.

She doesn't realize that the story of her and this man has just begun. That her grief, her panic, have stirred up something buried inside him that he can't give a name to, something hidden by all the certainties of Category II loners.

She goes home. Holes up in one corner of the living room. Makes herself very small. Pulls her knees up to her chest. The rest of the day will pass and she won't move. Fear. The rest of her life like this Sunday afternoon.

On Monday she doesn't go to work. Or the next day, or the next. There's food lying around, a stack of dirty dishes. Everything's upside down. She has taken the mirror off the wall, put it in front of her. She spends hours looking at herself, unseeing, now and then checks the progress of her decline. Doesn't wash, doesn't answer the phone, sleeps very little, in short bursts. At night, she lights candles by the mirror.

She has decided to have a breakdown. Decided it's better to find a medical term for her life instead of this gaping hole day after day, instead of this absence of everything, always, everywhere.

In a while someone will get worried, is bound to come and ask questions. Will persuade her to see someone. First she'll be stuffed with drugs, they'll make her sleep. She'll say a couple of things on some shrink's couch. They'll have her pick up her life. Something will have happened. A reference point: "The day I had my breakdown!" Her life will be reorganized around that statement. She'll stop resisting, she'll become fragile once and for all.

That staging doesn't match her personality. After a few days a powerful need regains the upper hand. A musty smell, a smell of rotting food floats in the apartment. She can't stand her greasy hair. The sun seeps through the closed blinds. Outside, the sandbars, the river, the air that's becoming milder, the first fine days of the season she's in the process of missing. Maybe her next breakdown will be successful. And as she has a horror of everything that rings false, she cleans, tidies, wipes away the signs of this nonsense. In the shower she thinks that her tragedy is this: always landing on her feet, with no extremes, no fuss, no drifting. When everything's in place again she goes back and sits by the mirror, which she hasn't hung. She misses you. Her image fills the whole space. Go to the café to be near you; she'd like that. Certain details in the painting have escaped her: your hands, the colour of your lips, the clothes under your unbuttoned coats.

A week has gone by when she shuts her apartment door. On the sidewalk, children wielding chalk are drawing African landscapes with animals. The neighbours are polishing their cars. The first really warm Sunday of the year. It's two p.m. She sighs; it's easier to live with her nightmares on a day like this.

At this time of day, and with the sun shining, the café is empty. The owner greets her. She sits near the painting. The trio forms again, but at the same time the harmony in the mirror no longer exists. She orders wine. When the owner comes to serve it, she asks if the painting is still stirring up enthusiasm and indignation. He tells her that the controversy has made it into the local paper, that his weekday business has gone up significantly. All in all, this whole business has meant fantastic publicity for him, and as the owner of a newly opened business, who's trying to build a loyal clientele, he couldn't ask for more. Now your anguish has become profitable. Maybe we'll soon find pictures, miniature replicas of the raft, on sale at the tourist stands near the wharves. She curses the age, asks for more wine.

What should she guess that she hasn't already guessed? What should she read into the painting? She lingers over all the details that had escaped her. Wants to leave here with the precise image, the exact expression of your faces. To summon you up at the blankest hours of the week she has to get through, wearing the skin of a reasonable little person.

A group of young people comes into the café. She leaves discreetly, the way one leaves a church. As the café is very close to the port, and because the Pinot Noir has completed the numbing of her grief, and since the humans she runs into on this late afternoon are smiling, she decides to go and greet the river and ask it, in passing, if there isn't another way than yours to launch an attack on the world.

On the docks she thinks that the river is a man, that she knows everything about him. His smell, his moods, his caresses, his setbacks. That she has never been able to imagine living any distance from this giant. That she has never imprinted those words on the body of a man.

Clinging to the raft, facing the café window, the two of you are observing her from a distance with the same dull gaze, the same strained smile. You are also watching the man from the café, who is quickening his pace just behind her — the man who, in a moment, will drop his words onto this woman's shoulders.

A meeting. He says things that are neither banal nor stupid. Doesn't try to charm her. A voice she could listen to for a long time. At once deep and light. She turns her head, sees the lines at the corners of his eyes, his weary look. She smiles as she answers him, because of the wine and the river in the background. She doesn't come on to him, doesn't think about the future, the past, doesn't wonder if her lipstick's worn off.

He asks an outsider's questions. She catches herself telling him all about crab-fishing, about the fate of the seals, the whales, the cod and, while she's at it, the World War II German submarines, shipwrecks throughout history, and about an artist who dropped thousands of ceramic figurines into the river. She talks incessantly. Tries to hold onto him. To see if anything's going to happen, if the two of them will fall to their knees, cradle each other's faces, tell each other, damp-eyed, that they've been waiting millions of years for this moment, ever since the day when, deep in the ocean, they felt in their crabs' bodies that one fine day they'd emerge, their carapaces would split, would become less rigid, that the road and the space they'd travel would bring them here to the dock in this town and then all their fatigue, all their solitude would melt like the ice on this river at the end of winter.

For the time being, a man and a woman, eyes glued to the river, dare not look at one another for fear of seeing in the other's eyes that nothing is happening.

Now they turn their backs to the river. Farther away, in the middle of the town, bells are ringing. At this hour, women are calling to children with dirty hands, with skinned knees.

She's surprised to have talked so much — it's not like her, she wishes she hadn't. Knows nothing about him. Not even his name. Slowly they climb towards the boulevard. As they go past the café she slows down, glances inside. You haven't budged. She thinks that one day she'll go into that café and only the river will be left in the painting. They fall silent. At the intersection of the boulevard, what comes next is decided easily, with no awkwardness. Each takes off in his own direction, he with his hands in his pockets, she with her nails digging into the leather strap on her bag.

They move away from one another. The street reveals its ugliness. The sky, the tattered clouds. The afternoon is dying to the sound of automobiles. All that's left of the Pinot Noir is a headache; of the man who's going away, only a vague anger. A body, a voice are getting away from her. Nothing remains in her hands. Tomorrow she'll go back to work. People will enquire about her health. She'll reply that she is serene, that things glide over her. That they needn't worry. That neither unhappiness nor happiness nor sickness has any claim on her. That they'll have their meticulous columns of figures before the ten o'clock break.

Perhaps he has stopped and is watching her walk away. Or maybe he's turned around; in a moment she'll hear his voice asking her name. She'll tell him she doesn't remember. They will laugh, set off again together. She is virtually immobilized on the sidewalk, has turned her head slightly, just enough to sense that there's no one behind her. Then she turns around. Sees him walking away with his hands in his pockets.

An act of daring. Madness. An irrepressible cry is about to burst out. To celebrate the irony of this afternoon, the night that will follow, this river and its reasonable blue that has been unable to stop time, the four marks on the leather strap, she cups her hands around her mouth and shouts. And because she doesn't know his name and because at this very moment she is shrinking, becoming a little girl on a well-worn sidewalk, she shouts as loud as she can:

"Mister, nobody's ever kissed me like you!"

He's too far away to hear her voice. So she repeats, to herself:

"Mister, nobody's ever kissed me.

"Mister, nobody.

"Mister."

All week she tells herself that next time she won't talk so much, will ask only a couple of brief, well-placed questions. Will let him open up. She knows that he'll come to the café. That there'll be no need to feign surprise. That they made this date at the very moment when they turned their backs.

She plays along. Gets her hair done, buys clothes. As if the ritual of seduction were going to loosen the knots that keep them from touching one another. But she doesn't feel excited.

He has sat down close to her on the banquette. His move caught her unawares. Though she wasn't expecting that he'd sit at another table, or even that he'd act surprised when he spotted her. She'd rehearsed his entrance in her head a hundred times: he walks in and without hesitation heads for her, sits down at her table, but on the chair opposite her. Why, all of a sudden, does she feel overwhelmed, almost on the verge of tears, just because he sat on the banquette instead of a chair?

She looks to the painting for help. You're holding one another tightly, you can't do anything for her.

She won't have to ask any questions. He starts from scratch. Introduces himself, says his name slowly as if to print it indelibly on her, as if he were afraid she wouldn't retain it. He reconfirms. Yes, he's new in town. He came here because he was asked to. For his work, temporarily. He doesn't give details. She doesn't push it.

Now he asks questions. Not the ones she expects. He looks at the painting and asks what she thinks of it. She recounts your story as the newspapers did, describes the controversy surrounding the painting.

"That's not it," he says. "I already know that part, tell me about the boys."

Those are the words needed to split the crabs' carapaces. Now things can happen between them. How can she explain it to him? They're no longer looking at the painting. They have turned to face one another. He waits for her to speak.

"I don't know what to tell you. I don't know why the tragedy of those two children has become the tragedy of the entire town and of everyone in it. I don't know why we've recognized them as our sons, our brothers, our gods. I don't know how to explain to you that they've become encrusted in our lives, have exacerbated the solitude of every one of us, have starved us, made us feel so guilty that we look down whenever we meet young men their age on the street. Look around you, look at the people in this café, look carefully, despite the hubbub around them, despite the luxury of butter and egg on their tongues, despite the comfort of coffee, look at them cast frightened glances at the picture; can you see that those boys aren't alone on the raft?"

A flight of lyricism. She came out with it in one breath. He wanted to know, now he'll know. He must think she's excessive, theatrical. He's not looking at her as if she were crazy. Finally gets around to asking her name.

Afterwards, the air is lighter. The waiter brings their trays. The man moves, takes the chair across from her, to make more room. The table is small and covered with their food. She sees again the three places set in the early morning.

He suggests the river, the tourist crossing. Almost apologizes for his invitation — one only a stranger would offer. Asks if the trip is worth doing. She tells him that the river never disappoints.

They leave the café, she feels out of place with her flimsy shoes, her new clothes, her perfume. Mismatched — that's the word that springs to mind when she sees their reflection in the window. Mismatched but together.

They meet men, women, families. They're one couple among others; this Sunday morning can turn out however it wants, can turn lighthearted or sour; the sky, the river can go on aspiring to the devastating beauty of their blue, she is walking beside a man who hasn't insisted on anything, hasn't asked her for anything yet, aside from this trip on the river, this crossing with no destination except the dock where their footsteps are already inscribed.

They won't be alone. Many people want to dissolve into the landscape.

They slip through. She leads him to the front of the boat. The passengers are elbowing their way. Everyone looks for a place in the front row. They stand there for a long while, not talking, leaning against one another because that's what the crowd has decided, because they don't want to disrupt this pause in their lives, this fragile moment when they'll have the impression as they pull away from shore that they no longer have to be wary of one another.

Eventually they give their places to a family with very young children who are growing impatient, who are despairing of ever seeing any seals. They stand off to one side.

There's a festive atmosphere on deck. Children. Numerous and of every age. Paying attention to the landscape that surrounds them, or else totally uninterested. Adults buy them ice cream, blow their noses, hold them by the hand. Their fine hair in this light, the white skin of their faces, their tiny fingers.

Her suspicion flares up all at once.

"Do you have children?" she asks abruptly, a way of asking whether somewhere else, on another planet, he might by chance be hiding another life that resembles those before their eyes. So she can know now, right away, whether there's some trap she may have missed. So she can prepare her reply for when he tells her that she's a wonderful interlude in his life.

"Yes, a fifteen-year-old son I don't see very often. What about you?"

He has tossed the question back quickly. As if to avoid pursuing it any further.

She answers no. The urge to add that if she did, she wouldn't be here on a Sunday afternoon, on the docks or in the café, would not be here with him but in the middle of the deck with the others, she wouldn't be wearing these ridiculous shoes and dress but jeans smeared with ice cream, her pockets would be full of soggy Kleenex, she'd keep running her fingers through her children's fine hair.

In her head, an echo: a fifteen-year-old son. Time passes. As if the river that encircles her were reminding her of it. A boy of fifteen. A segment of her life. Precisely that part where, every minute of every day, she has dug at the ground with her fingernails to implant her quest, to bury her pain. To find the key or the treasure. A fifteen-year-old son, the way you say a fifteen-metre hole in the ground, a fifteen-year-long blank space in her head.

They're such strangers to one another, it's palpable. She wishes there were a set of instructions she could take out of her purse and consult. She wishes it were as it was in her childhood: when someone she didn't know asked her questions she couldn't answer, she'd turn anxiously to her mother, who would take over. The answers she hadn't given had flowed readily, lightly from her mother's mouth. A fifteen-year-old son he doesn't see. That's not an answer, it's a wound. How many other wounds are hidden beneath his tired, peaceful manner? How many other confessions like that would he offer up to her with great effort? And in the sum of their respective wounds, which of the two piles would turn out to be higher?

Around her, nothing but strangers. The gestures, the words they exchange. The concern they show one another. She would sell her soul to the devil to have someone suddenly appear there on the deck, someone she knows, someone who loves her.

Across from them, a very young child is sleeping on his father's shoulder.

"My son is severely handicapped," he lets drop.

Then, looking over at the sleeping child:

"Children take up whatever room there is."

She would like to say something, add that even the children one doesn't have can sometimes take up whatever room there is. The words don't come. He senses her discomfort, smiles:

"All right, we'll keep the chapter of wounds and injuries for later."

The boat is approaching the other shore. He's surprised

not to spot any village, only the dock, the road. A thirty-minute stop is announced.

He's said something that refers to the future. *Later*: that's the word she holds onto. So there will be a continuation, other secrets to reveal. He will tell, she will listen, with her face very close to his. The lines around his eyes, his greying temples will become familiar, appealing. Her only response will be to run her hand over his face. One day, perhaps, he'll say to her: "Make me forget." And she'll reply: "Give me a memory."

Now that the boat has docked, they'll walk along the road. Most of the passengers making the round trip also disembark. The children, confined to the scenery and the deck for an hour and a half, run off in every direction. The adults stretch, get the kinks out of their legs. The party continues. He says that they all look as if they're stepping onto terra firma after sailing for months, that they're docking at an unknown island, that they've just left Noah's Ark, that they're going home after spending nine months wandering the flooded earth. He has spread his arms as if to welcome the landscape, the new life. She watches him laugh. All at once the desire to move closer, to touch him, to link arms with him. To tell him that she'd like this to continue, that she no longer knows the formulas to untie the knots, that she doesn't know how to make things work so they'll last, so she won't find herself, at the end of the day, watching him walk away along the sidewalk.

The other passengers have stayed near the dock. Now they're alone on the road. Her heels keep getting stuck in the grooves in the broken pavement, and when she walks on the side of the road they sink into the gravel.

"It's because of the nine months at sea, you've forgotten how to walk on terra firma!"

He goes on laughing, looks at her as if he knows her. On his face there is something she can't name. The first feeling that comes when a person suddenly stops being a stranger. A sign of recognition.

The word *temporarily* looms up, and at the same time mistrust, the empty years, the men who didn't stay, the birthdays of other people's children, the two digits of her age rise to the surface. If he remains part of her life, they won't be starting from scratch, won't take the place of those couples holding children by the hand. If this man stays in her life it will be to grow old along with her. They won't have time for children, his body too will fail him, it's inscribed on the wrinkles and circles under his eyes, on the veins that protrude at his wrists. What she's expecting won't happen. She knows that now, everything around her repeats it: the children on the dock, the river in the definitive blue of this Sunday afternoon, the tired shoulders of the man walking beside her. She thinks that the people around them don't see them as an odd couple. Young couples look at them and think that their children no longer spend Sunday afternoons with them, perhaps even envy them their freedom from family constraints.

The boat is heading back. On the deck, you'd swear someone had administered tranquillizers to all the passengers, particularly the children. They've all found a place to sit down: on the benches, the ground, on every part of the boat they can lean on. The party's over.

They've settled in at the back of the boat. She has taken off her shoes. Her heels are flayed. What would he say if she threw the shoes overboard? A way of warning him that you never know with her, that small incidents of weird behaviour are also a way of confiding secrets when the words are stuck in your throat.

He forces open the door. Asks her to talk about her childhood. She describes the sandbars as a place for games and treasure washed up on shore. The light, the colour, the beauty, the air. The river's hold on her frail new life. She feels the first knot coming undone. She speaks slowly, feels as if she's hearing another woman's voice and at the same time, oddly enough, her own voice as a small child. She speaks more quietly, closes her eyes. As if she's been given a tranquillizer too. She goes on. Talks about the river inside the child, of its first movements, of the hope those movements carry inside them. She talks about time, which doesn't exist for the child; about the sky that stretches to infinity above its head. By the end, she senses that her small voice is trying to go back deep in her chest. Just before she loses her voice, and not knowing if it will ever come back, she starts to sing. An old song she's known forever. A song about a shipwreck, about sailors lost at sea, about tearful sweethearts. All around them is a religious silence; the children have looked up, people are listening to her. More knots are coming undone. Madness, the soothing variety.

It's five o'clock when the boat enters the harbour. The hour for finding the words for holding on. She hopes he'll be the one who says them. For once, let someone say to her: "Stay with me" or "I'm keeping you here" or "Don't go." Let someone cling to her as to a raft. A raft. Your image rises in her at the same time as her fears. Fear of the boulevard a few hundred metres away, fear of reliving the scene from last Sunday, of seeing herself in thirty years, on the docks, late Sunday afternoon, alone with the river and her memories of sand inscribed on the palms of her hands.

One of her heels breaks. As if her fear were suddenly too heavy. She takes off her shoes, in one falsely casual movement tosses them away, to give the impression that nothing has any importance, even though she's scared to death, barefoot on the rough pavement. She tells herself that he can't leave her now, she's too vulnerable, her shoes have spoken in her place. He won't be able to tell her that he enjoyed the day just before he turns his back on her. He leads her to the café. She's won.

Without consulting one another, on a shared impulse,

they go to a table in front of the painting. They sit side by side on the banquette. Her fear dissolves. She smiles at the two of you as if it were you who had just taken it away. The floor of the restaurant is cold, she tucks her legs under her thighs.

"Look," he says, "they're like you, they aren't wearing shoes either."

That detail had escaped her. It looks strange, especially because they're warmly dressed.

"Painter's oversight," she replies.

"Why?"

"Because they can't have taken their shoes off on the raft. It must have been freezing cold on the river that night. It's surprising he didn't paint them. Look, he could just as well have drawn the cap that was found. Did you know that a sailboat brought back one of their caps?"

"Yes."

"You do? Were you already here last October?"

"No."

"But you still know. . . ."

"Yes. In fact, the artist may have painted the boys just as they were starting to get undressed. People who commit suicide by drowning sometimes relieve themselves of their clothing."

"They got undressed? How can anyone know that?"

"They don't. I meant in general."

"Do you know a lot about drowning?"

"Not about drowning, but I do know something about suicide."

"Are you an investigator?"

"No, a psychiatrist."

The word lands like a bomb.

Perhaps he's been spying on her from the beginning? Perhaps he's analysed every one of her mannerisms, her words, her tone of voice, the expression on her face? Perhaps he's already read everything, seen everything: her poverty, her quest, the small fissures, her loneliness?

Perhaps he's even guessed at the presence of the boys deep in the mirror? Perhaps he's filed her as a specific type? Has he seen symptoms in her that reveal some dysfunction? Perhaps he already knows that her persistent appetite and her fervour are never able to reverse steam, to fill all the blank spaces in her head? Perhaps he knows that, unlike him, she doesn't carry around a drama as heavy as lead? That her life is something tepid, uninteresting?

She's stopped talking. Dug her heels in. Feels herself become transparent. Disappointment, anger. She drains her glass of wine in one gulp. After a moment of silence, he asks:

"Is it dangerous to be sitting beside a shrink?"

"Why did you come here to practise?"

He points to the painting:

"Because of them. Their suicide set off a shock wave in the population. Related cases started appearing right after they disappeared. A few weeks later they reached a level that alarmed the medical community. When it happened, one of the hospital psychiatrists had just retired. I was asked to come; they were afraid they'd be overwhelmed. I've always been interested in this kind of situation. Which is getting back to normal, as a matter of fact."

"What kinds of cases?" she asks quietly, somewhat reluctantly, as if there's a risk she'll hear him describing her.

"Anxiety, guilt, panic attacks, thoughts of suicide, a few attempts. This town hasn't finished mourning yet. The people I see have been overwhelmed by what happened; and those boys are still there. Take this painting, for instance. You know very well what I mean, you've felt it yourself. You told me a while ago, when I asked you what effect those boys have on you."

"I suppose that was my first session?"

An aggressive remark. After the boys and her childhood, what more does he want from her? That she lie down on the banquette? That she give him a detailed description of the mirror, Christmas night, the three places set at the table, the whole winter with the boys taking shelter at her place? Their presence supporting her, restraining her? And then if that's not enough, for the same price, the week when she dropped out, hoping for a breakdown?

He's laid his hand on her arm. A first move. He tells her that nobody's safe from images. Shrinks no more than anyone else. And then he adds more solemnly, attempting to get through to her, that the young men he's treating, the ones he sees on the street, even the two across from them in the painting, are a constant reminder of what could have happened some distance away, of another young man neither dead nor alive who spends most of the time strapped to a bed or a chair. To each his ghosts.

They've finished the half-bottle of Pinot, making small talk. They don't touch again. Don't move closer together. Their crab carapaces have grown back. In spite of them. A moment later he gets up, says he's parked nearby, he'll go and get the car since she doesn't have shoes.

Before they've even left the port area, he says in a neutral voice:

"I'm leaving in a week."

Not in a week, she thinks, but in ten minutes, when he stops the car at her door. Time is short. She could ask him in, even if their desire isn't equal to their expectations, even if despite their efforts the barriers haven't come down — either that or they've put up new ones, or at least she has.

She replies by telling him which way to go. They drive along the boulevard, with the river on one side. They don't say anything more.

They've arrived. He parks, leaves the engine running. Knots. What should she say? That it's been a fantastic day? That she hopes his return to his usual life goes well, with lots of fascinating cases? That his face, the lines on it, his tired shoulders will stay imprinted in her somewhere? That she'll think of him sometimes, when she senses a void and the onset of weird behaviour?

He leans over, rummages in the glove compartment. Pencil, scrap of paper. Hands her his phone number.

"A week, if you feel like it."

She shuts the door, turns around. A last wave. He drives off. From the sidewalk, she watches him disappear.

III

THE BREAKING OF THE WATERS

The bedroom window is open. The curtains are drawn. Their slight movement. The light that she assumes is there. She hears birds, cars. Down below, the boys' voices, the familiar sounds of breakfast. A day is beginning. She keeps her eyes closed. With her body curled up under the covers, she's on strike. Won't be there for anyone. Not for the boys, who'll forget their lunch bags; not for the girl, who'll forget that she exists; not for her husband, not for the squirrels. For none of them. She'll get up after they've all gone. A way of marking the distance, of telling them to leave some air for her. A lie. A way of yet again not noticing her relentless struggle to resist their indifference.

Doors slam. Her husband comes to tug her out of her false sleep. He sits on the edge of the bed. At his feet, a suitcase. Business trip. A few moments later, the sound of a car door, the rumble of an engine. Then silence, the empty house. She can get up.

She doesn't notice the closed door to the girl's room before she starts down the stairs. Outside, the dog is scratching to be let in. In the messy kitchen the radio is sputtering its idiotic songs.

A sight to behold: there she is in the middle of the kitchen, in her torn, shapeless old bathrobe, just before the sky falls on her head, just before she finds the letter no one's noticed, hidden under the cereal box and addressed to her in a wobbly little hand that she recognizes right away.

As she tears open the envelope, she already knows that the letter is going to blow up in her hands. The words fall into line in her head, one by one. Short sentences try to explain, to reassure, to avoid wounding. Time stops: it can't be her daughter, this isn't her letter, it's not her, the mother. The words in the letter leave her head, hurl themselves at her heart. Pain in her chest, her pulse racing. And then they take refuge in the hollow of her belly.

The stairs four at a time. The girl's room, perfectly tidy. Some clothes are missing from the dresser drawers: T-shirts, socks, underwear. A confirmation, the first one. In the kitchen, the letter left behind on the table. The coffee, the bread, the orange juice. On the windowsill, the squirrel. The dog's head through the screen door he's just torn.

She goes outside. As if to look for signs, as if the nightmare were going to be erased. Around her, the garden, the trees, the warmth of a June morning.

She comes back to the table. The letter. For once, her daughter speaks. But no revelation, no secret. The girl's words: *travel, need, change of air*. She starts to tremble. Feels sick to her stomach. Her own words: *departure, runaway, danger, loss*. She tries to calm down, nearly succeeds, recapitulates. Her daughter has gone. Only she knows. The boys are at school, her husband is on a highway somewhere. What alarm must she sound? Pull herself together. That's what counts. Remember the movements that mean control. She tidies the kitchen, makes more coffee, feeds the squirrel, lets the dog in.

She pulls on some clothes, not the ones she'd have worn if nothing had happened. Something presentable, in case she has to go out in a hurry. Fixes her hair, puts on makeup. She's ready for any eventuality.

She turns the kitchen into her headquarters. Has set the phone on the table. Next to it, her address book, paper, a pencil. She waits.

She hasn't noticed yet that you have disappeared

from the door of the fridge.

Needs confirmation that her daughter has gone. What if she phoned the school? The thought puts her off. That would be sounding the alarm. The police? That would mean making the drama official. How would she explain: "Good morning, it's ten a.m., a few hours ago my daughter left to go somewhere, I'm calling to report that she's disappeared." It's too soon to believe in it, too soon to act. And then she senses vaguely that there's something else. In her hands, the envelope addressed to her: it's between the two of them. And as there's no longer very much between them, this journey, this running away, makes them collaborators.

The minutes pass. She's proud. Doesn't cry, has stopped trembling. In any case, the hour of danger hasn't sounded yet. The day is young, the light is intruding into every nook and cranny of the world. At this very moment human beings everywhere are occupying space. Streets, alleys, vacant lots. All the places that, once night has fallen, will terrorize her. For the time being, she must gather her strength, try to understand, design a strategy. It will take a long time. She looks at the clock: "This is going to go on for hours." She emphasizes the word *hours*, suppresses the others. *Days, nights, weeks.*

The image of your mother has come up naturally. A thin little woman, sitting at a kitchen table just as she herself is, holding a crumpled sheet of paper. Her discreet tears, the way her shoulders move, the flowered cotton dress. Each time the same image, the same anguish because this is happening to her. Today that woman is a sister.

Her eyes light on the door of the fridge.

The white square, empty. The precise spot where your photo was. All around, other messages, photos, notices. She jumps up. Feels a pounding in her chest. Looks on the floor, the counters, in the garbage can; shifts the fridge. Your photo can't be found. Someone has taken it, carried it away. The boys? No, they haven't been touched by the young men's gazes. Her husband? Maybe. He's had enough of their morbid presence, wants to turn the page. But why today, just before leaving?

And what if it was the girl? What should she conclude from that? Is it possible that day after day, for months now, the young men have been appealing to her, inviting her to join them? That every time she made the banal gesture of opening the fridge to take out some food, the girl got that appeal right in her face, like a supplication? Could it be that you have betrayed her, the mother who felt a blind affection for you and placed you at the heart of her bright kitchen?

Someone's taken away the photo. Perhaps the girl. Probably. The two of you have taken her daughter away. To the state of emergency is now added a declaration of war.

At noon she turns on the radio. Local news, no tragedy to report. She breathes.

In the kitchen she remains sitting. Early afternoon, the sun is warm, lethargy creeps into all things, freezes them in the light. Appearances are deceiving, she thinks. While in here time seems suspended, the distance the girl has travelled is growing at a dizzying rate, every second making the gap between them bigger. Where is she right now? She speaks her name, calls it out — it's like an incantation — just trying to calm herself, to bring the girl back to her.

The only response is the irregular breathing of the dog lying on the floor in a shaft of light. In her hands, the letter, hard as rock.

One question remains. How far back would she need to go to locate the first silence, the first absent gaze that would lead to all the others? In what chapter of childhood are they hiding? The ceremony of the images files past, memories buried, lost, yet all at once more alive than ever.

And the final silence? The one that ordered the girl's departure, the one that she, the mother, suffered, the one that meant her downfall, how did it escape her perspicacity? Over the course of the months just gone by, all she saw was typical adolescent anxiety: touching, ridiculous and temporary. She stood back, her arms open — as always — children never go away very far or for very long, she told herself. Liar, liar, she told herself repeatedly as well.

The phone rings. Shock, adrenalin. An expression of friendship, a request for news. A casual enquiry as to how she's doing. Her reply, lying again. Her gaze fixed intensely on the blank white square in the middle of the fridge door.

The two of you, at this hour, are far away, hidden somewhere among the rocks on the sandbars. You've left this bright kitchen the way someone escapes from prison. Breathless, leaning against one another, young deserters, you're surprised to discover that sometimes the gods too are stifled by normal affection.

The boys will be home from school soon. They'll be wound up, today's the last day of school. A tornado, the place taken over. She hasn't left the kitchen since this morning. She holds the letter, knows the worst is yet to come. On the walls, the light shifts, changes colour, shows her that in the end night will follow day. And then her hell will begin.

Memories loom up. Childhood, her own. Scant images. Boredom, impatience. Childhood like an enclave to be fled. The very site of deprivation, drought and poverty. Grow up, grow old, the watchword continued to resonate. She quickly became a girl without memory. Very young, she wanted a child. Suspected that it would make up for everything; that childhood would be given back to her on a silver platter; that she would shape it however she wanted, and the magic word *happiness* would be inscribed on the backs of photos to be care-

fully placed in albums. And she was right: childhood
had been restored to her, with all its music. The children,
one after another, had touched her face with their little
hands. She'd learned affectionate gestures for respond-
ing to them. The world had been put back in order.
Finally, the bone stuck in her throat since her birth had
been removed. The party could begin. Expert and awkward, she confirmed that it was possible to reinvent the
world.

She has put her feet on the chair, drawn her knees up
to her chest, put her arms around her legs. She wasn't
right about everything. Today the music has stopped.
And even when the boys come home in a few minutes, it
won't start up again.

Perhaps she'd imposed on them a ready-made childhood, the one she'd have liked to have. Perhaps she
hadn't seen the childhood her daughter had forged for
herself, silently, patiently, in the secrecy of her room. Her
laughter, her songs had taken up too much room, had
created the enclave where, for want of anything better,
the girl had taken refuge. Today she has broken down
the walls.

First, loud voices on the sidewalk; then the racket of
the slamming door, school bags pitched onto the floor.
The kitchen invaded, the boys raiding the fridge. Recon-
struct her character. She won't have to wait all alone now;
she hides the letter in her pocket, clears the table, puts
the phone back on the wall. "Everything all right, boys?"
And then, in a detached tone of voice, asks if they've
taken the photo off the fridge. "What photo?" They tear
out the back door, a soccer ball under one arm, the dog
following them, glad to be leaving the kitchen.

It's five o'clock. She'll have to provide a meal for the
boys. Put up with their frenzy till ten o'clock. After that,
once they're in bed, she'll be alone with the letter again.

When she moves, her whole body aches. Perfectly
ordinary movements, everyday objects heavier than

rocks. The boys will eat early and quickly; it's a beautiful day, they'll go back outside for the evening. The smell of food turns her stomach, she wonders if her daughter has eaten today.

Now, her certainty that the girl won't come home from school. The wave of the last buses and the latecomers on foot with their backpacks has just gone by. In the street the atmosphere is festive because summer holidays are beginning. Her concern will grow, will make her crazy by midnight. She clings to the words in the letter, which she knows by heart. A journey, a real one, with buses, sidewalks in a bigger town, youth hostels. To see those images, only those.

At the table, the boys are eating. She leaves them alone, walks out of the room. She's decided to phone. Couldn't bear the reproaches. Feels terrorized at the thought of hearing her own voice: "Our daughter's gone and she's left a letter." Hundreds of kilometres away, another voice tells her that her husband hasn't checked into the hotel yet. She gives her name, leaves a message but indicates that it isn't urgent. A reprieve. Just a little more time for her and the girl. Just a little more time before she betrays her. For she's well aware that eventually she'll sound the alarm, that all her nightmares will finally win the day, by being stronger than the invisible link between her and the girl at this moment.

A breathing space. The boys went out as soon as they'd bolted their meal. She does the dishes, persists in clinging to those actions that make her feel the ground beneath her feet is still solid. It's six o'clock. She turns on the TV. Images of Bosnia: a mass grave, women looking on as bodies are exhumed — bones, skulls, leather shoes — where is their child? At the end of the news, as if to lighten the weight of the world, there's an item about a cat that saved her kittens from a Brooklyn building in flames. Clumsily, blinded by smoke, the mother put her babies down one by one on the sidewalk across the street.

Offers of adoption have poured in by the hundreds.

How many images will never be filmed? All those women haunted by the same obsessive fear, the same terror in the face of loss. Every time, a single enemy to fight. She thinks, the little woman in the flowered dress has also watched the news. She'll never be part of those images, never be the short-lived star of some TV news broadcast. Her story belongs to silence, her silhouette facing the river will always be anonymous.

She turns off the TV. Usually she feels a guilty relief at the end of the news. As if each time she is being told that, today, she's been spared again. Tonight, however, the voices of the world won't bring her any help.

She has to go back to the girl's room. She can't help herself. All day she's forbidden herself to do it. For fear of betraying secrets, of stumbling over truths that are too harsh. She turns the doorknob very slowly. She's done it often, so as not to disturb the girl as she sleeps. At this time of day the light in the room turns all her certainties upside down. Even as a child, the girl liked to isolate herself in her room, particularly at this time of day. Just after the evening meal, just before the ritual of sleep that began with her bath. All at once her dizziness returns. The room is perfectly neat and tidy. How many times has she reprimanded her for scattering her clothes all over, for leaving books and crumpled notebooks on the floor? Now everything is in its place; not one crease on the bed, none of her belongings lying around. The soft light on the furniture makes the room even more terrifying. As if the girl, by carefully putting everything away, wanted to leave a second message: "You see this room, you see I no longer exist."

The absence of clues, of signs, leaves her desolate. There is nothing that lets her imagine the girl during the final moments before she left. And what if a year from now, or five years or ten, the room has remained intact and nothing has moved? She leans against the wall. No, it isn't time for the official search. Later, when hope is exhausted, she'll come back to scrutinize minutely every drawer, every notebook. Just as she's about to shut the door one detail keeps her there. There's a cassette in the Walkman. It must be the last one she listened to before she left. She sits on the bed, fits the earphones over her ears. The music doesn't give her any answers.

She's gone back downstairs, blessing the fact that the days are so long at this time of year. She goes from room to room, doesn't know what to do, doesn't know how to stop moving. Finally she goes out to the garden, leaving the door open behind her so she can hear the phone. The warmth of the air is soothing. All around her, the plants reveal their touching fragility. Now, in early summer, the colours haven't faded yet. From the street come children's voices. Not a leaf moves. Insects, many of them, fly in the light and seem mad: they dart back and forth as if they're constantly banging into invisible walls. "That's it, that's what youth is, to be swept along into the light," she catches herself saying out loud. She stands there, not moving, observing the scene, freed of all the movements she's forced on herself since the boys came home from school.

The garden — the limits of the world. For a long time it was equal to the task. The girl spent a solitary childhood there between the sandbox and the swing set. Sometimes neighbourhood children came. Later, the girl had put up a tent where she spent most of her time in the summer, sleeping there whenever it didn't rain. Then one day the boys stormed the garden with their noisy games, their friends. Dislodged, the girl readily laid down her arms. She wasn't seen in the garden again. That was the period when her door was closed all year long.

Where is she now? At this precise moment, whose gaze is alighting on the red highlights in her hair, kindled there by the sun? On what place in the world has her own sad gaze touched down?

Furtively, the two of you have come back to her. Hidden in the foliage, you spy on her. Huddled on the steps, she keeps running her hands over her face, as if to waken herself from a bad dream. Curious and ill at ease, you observe her; you didn't expect that the thin little woman in the flowered dress would reappear here, in this garden, that she would borrow another body, another face. No one warned you that memory survives the worst disasters. You guess at all her fears, you have all the answers. You'll reveal nothing. You abandon her to her doubts; the gods are merely an infinitely light breath in the foliage.

Her thoughts betray her. She wishes she could control them, reason with them. Would like it if action plans suggested themselves and blocked the strange roads down which her mind is drifting. For example, when she wonders, "What kind of mother should I be when she comes back?" she wishes the responses were laid down in the psychology books she should have read. But the image that wells up, on the contrary, destroys everything: she sees herself very old and gaunt, lying in a bed; her body feels as if it weighs a ton; her bones crack, constantly seem about to fracture; she can see and hear reasonably well. A middle-aged woman — her daughter — comes up to her and asks if she recognizes her. How can she not guess at her perfume, the fatigue in her voice, the wear and tear in her gaze? Nervously the woman rearranges the covers. Asks if she's eaten well, slept well, if her brothers have come to visit her lately. From deep in her bed she replies with little motions of her head. The woman won't ask the other questions, won't ask whether life is long, whether death makes her panic, won't offer a word of regret, of memories, of all the time behind them. Twenty minutes later, she'll put on her coat and, kissing her forehead, say too loudly: "See you next Sunday!"

At other moments the reel of images runs backwards.

She sees herself at fifteen. From her classroom window she can catch a glimpse of the river in the distance. A fine rain is falling on the town. The autumn afternoon goes on and on, interminably. Soon the bell will announce a weekend even greyer and longer than the week that's just gone by. As she walks home slowly, despite the rain, she dreams about going away, about leaving everything, here, now. She dreams about entering her life through all the doors that she doesn't know, that are hidden from her. She imagines other places very far from this town, in particular very far from this river that stands before her like the bars of a prison. Her one certainty: the river is a breaker of dreams.

She didn't go away, has never left the town. When she was young and pregnant and a house became necessary, she insisted that it be in the part of town farthest from the river, away from its spray and its odours. Later, when she had to give in to the children and she found herself on the sandbar, carting shovels and buckets, building castles from the clayey sand, its law struck, impalpable. It was she who went to get the water and they, the children, never went past the wrack line left by the tide. As if the world had just two truths: the river's, elusive and abhorrent, and the coastline's, which could be moulded in the palms of one's hands. She thinks that she isn't unhappy now, and hasn't been during all these years. Finally entered her life through just one door. The others stayed shut. Though she tells herself that her life is full, that it's overflowing all around her, all those closed doors in front of her keep her from breathing. And then she imagines her daughter getting off a bus, stepping into a strange town and taking a deep breath. The picture makes her smile.

At this precise moment you know that, on the deck of a boat, a girl is holding her breath as she discovers that the river is a breaker of dreams.

The light fades. The sun has set behind the trees and

houses. It's about to throw itself into the river. How to summon her courage, how to silence the voice that tells her again and again that she hasn't understood a thing? Her daughter will come back. That's the sentence she has to pour into her head, minute by minute.

TV images still appear before her eyes. What she knows of the world has come to her just from her screen, she knows that. One day, a story moved her to tears. It took place in France. An elderly man and woman had been waiting for their son for six years. He'd gone away at twenty, with some baggage, leaving no explanation. They'd found an empty bedroom, neat and tidy, as she had today. And so the parents — not concerned but surprised, thinking it was a lingering adolescent whim — had begun their docile wait. He didn't come back. They'd questioned his friends and acquaintances. No one had noticed anything. The timid and reserved young man hadn't given any sign, hadn't let drop any clue. Dread had come then, devastating dread, and had finally given way to an enormous, silent grief mixed with the persistence of expectation. She listened religiously as they told their story. But even more than the account of their drama, one small detail had overwhelmed her. The old couple were convinced that their son had taken his key when he left. Whenever they went out they slipped a tiny rolled-up piece of paper into the keyhole. It informed the young man that they wouldn't be long, begged him to wait for them. They only went out to do their shopping. When they came home and slowly climbed the five storeys of their building, carrying packages that were too heavy for their arms, a fierce hope, a fervent faith hammered at their temples. And every time, it ended the same way. The little piece of yellow paper still in the keyhole. The old couple retrieved the message and entered the apartment, resigned. The report ended with the door closing softly.

That's what panics her most. If the girl doesn't come

home she'll still have to do her shopping, carry packages, wait in the broken light of evening, give in to sleep,
despite herself, through an instinct for survival.

Suddenly, out of nowhere, the dog appears at the
back of the garden. As soon as he sees her he races over
to her. The boys follow. They sit down beside her. They're
hot. She looks at them intensely. They too will fall silent
eventually, avoid her eyes. They too will wish they could
tear up their childhood. Adolescence has already entered
them. Candour has been erased from their faces, their
arms are too long and it seems to her that the older boy's
voice is husky. Perhaps when their turn comes she'll
know what pains them, will be able to find the words,
the gestures. But above all she knows that nothing and
no one will be able to do anything about it. That there
will always be secret, hidden places for constructing rafts,
and that all the vigilance in the world will only serve to
provide them with the tools to build them.

The dog rests his head against her leg. It's nearly dark.
The boys went inside a while ago and she can hear the
horrible music from their video game. "Better go inside,"
she says to the dog, as if he were the only one who knew
everything, who had shared everything since morning.
As if it went without saying that he'd be there at her side
throughout the long night that was looming.

Just before closing the door, she is struck by the smell
of seaweed. The river sends it all the way here, tells her
that your photo is missing from the fridge, reminds her
that you, the two of you, did it. That perhaps the girl did
it too, despite the words in her letter that are meant to be
reassuring.

In the kitchen, the boys have left the bread, cookies
and milk out on the table. She's hungry. Never has she
detested herself as she does now.

The dog follows her into the living room. The video
game stops. The boys shout good night from the top of
the stairs. She hears herself answer them. Her voice is

cheerful. How does she do it? she wonders. She hates herself even more. She's cold. Refuses to shut the window. That would cut her off from the world. No cry, no call would reach her. She gets a blanket and settles herself on the sofa. In front of her, the TV set, time for the news. She won't turn it on. Tonight she won't sympathize with anyone's misfortunes. Let them go on dying in Chechnya or the Gaza Strip, let the blood flow, let the eyes of Somali children close once and for all, she doesn't give a damn. She holds tight in her hand a letter that's a grenade about to explode. And the world doesn't turn so quickly when you're holding a grenade in your hand.

PART THREE

GETTING BACK TO SHORE

Tomorrow, the solstice, first day of summer holidays. Children's cries will cover the town. For two months we will revel in those cries. The parks, the sidewalks will be taken over; bicycles will criss-cross the streets. It will be like a grand celebration. The town will also see the arrival of its annual batch of tourists.

For the time being, though, the night seems strangely calm. The wind has dropped. Now and then a car in the distance, its sound muffled. And the silent river. Its breathing extinguished, as in a state of apnea.

The cathedral clock chimes three. You've chosen this precise moment to say no for the second time: you will never be the gods of this town, or the gods of anywhere else, for that matter. You are turning your backs on eternity as you did on life eight months ago. You will go back to the river, you'll leave this place for good, you'll leave all these humans to themselves. Tomorrow morning they won't know why but they'll wake up lighter, less alone and, finally, not so guilty. They'll remember nothing but a vague mishap that cast a shadow over the town. They'll celebrate the return of summer, they'll breathe deeply as they stand facing the river, hands on hips. And you'll no longer be there. Swept away, you'll follow the path of your bodies, you'll arrive at the gulf and then the ocean will finish dissolving you. You will at last achieve your goal. All this will have been merely a detour, a temporary hitch. You'll have failed at your task. Will have survived neither human grief nor the implacable austerity of the gods. In fact, you know now that no destiny was decreed for you. Becoming a god turned out to be a cruel game. You couldn't live up to all the demands. You didn't understand how the game worked. When, in a burst of compassion, you leaned forward to console someone, he pulled back, burrowed away into his solitude; but then, when he begged you on bended knee to listen to him, you placed a mirror in front of his face. And from this you concluded that gods and humans are incompatible. The game became such a burden on your shoulders. The same sensation, the same heaviness had made you head out to sea on your raft.

You made your decision some time ago. On a sudden impulse. And if you're still wandering the streets of this town, and the wharves tonight, it's because there persists in you a remnant of curiosity, a bit of regard for a few humans who came closer to you than the others.

You didn't want to miss anything. At eleven o'clock you had to be everywhere at once: on the wharves, leaning against the sheds, behind a girl standing erect and motionless as a tree; in an apartment where a woman stands close to a telephone and a mirror, gripping a piece of paper with a man's phone number on it, her gaze fixed on the keypad, wondering if there's such a thing as paralysis of the heart, like that of the body; and somewhere else in the town, on a living-room sofa with all the lights out, next to a woman huddled under a blanket. Their grief is the only thing you want to take away, to dissolve it along with yourselves. A god's final act, a very small redemption, to prove that once, just once, you were right.

The boys have been in bed for several hours now. She's cold, tense under the blanket. She's put her watch on the table behind the sofa. Now time will be an enemy; all the watches and clocks in the world can stop, can shatter, time has taken refuge in her chest, at the very centre of the anguish that is breaking her, that will break her more with every second. She's given careful thought to everything she knows about the girl and it's not enough, a mystery is escaping her, the one key she needs is lost. She feels as if she took a sledgehammer blow to the back of her head this morning, and is only feeling the effects in the first hours of darkness tonight. She doesn't move, isn't aware of her heartbeat, her breathing seems to have stopped. She's worn out, has spent the day looking for her daughter in all the hidden corners of her life. She closes her eyes, numb, drained. There will be no cry, only mute, insidious uneasiness that eats away slowly, almost without her knowing. She brings her hand to her neck, her dizziness fills the space.

That gesture with her hand unsettles you. Somewhere in your memory is buried the same gesture made by the thin little woman in the flowered dress — your mother. Tonight you feel that your suffering was not wiped out at the moment when you were swallowed up by the black water of the river. Suffering is unsinkable. It can't be drowned, it can only be transferred to another body. Yours has taken shelter in the thin body of that little woman and, because the two of you had only one mother, her pain is twice as great, twice as heavy as the entire volume of the water in the river.

She won't give in to sleep. That would mean betraying, letting go of the girl's hand. She promises herself that she'll sleep as little as possible for as long as her daughter isn't there. In a few hours she'll sound the alarm, draw up a strategy. First she'll make enquiries of the girl's few friends and acquaintances. She'll also search her room from top to bottom, check with the hospital to see if during the night a girl. . . . And then, finally, she'll inform the police. That is no doubt what has to be done, in order or disorder, it hardly matters. And then she'll have to put up with the horde of the compassionate who'll want to support her in her ordeal. She'll miss her solitude, this strange rendezvous with her daughter.

A little later, when the dog who's been asleep on the carpet by the sofa raises his head all at once, his ears moving like antennae, when a shadow slips past behind the curtains, when the doorknob can be heard slowly turning, she knows that there'll be no triumph, just a kind of relief in her body that can't wipe out the pain deep in her chest.

The door opens with unreal slowness. Not one of her muscles moves. She stays wrapped in her blanket, tense in the extreme. Her eyes, accustomed to the dark for hours now, can make out everything. The girl comes inside, carrying nothing, no baggage, no coat. There's only the white of her T-shirt and her skin. All around her, a black hole. The girl shuts the door, stands in the entrance for a moment, motionless, surprised. As if the darkness inside the house, the calm that prevails there were impossible. The dog goes up to the girl, who finally notices the dark mass squeezed into one end of the sofa. She waits for it to talk. This doesn't happen, an unexpected scenario. She goes upstairs to the little blue room and locks the door, as usual.

On the sofa there is death or rebirth, she's not sure

which. She thinks about an article she read about transplant patients who, after the operation, at the fateful moment when they waken, are incredulous to rediscover the unbelievable noise of their own heartbeat, which they'd stopped hearing because of the weariness of the old muscle that's just been removed. It must be like the noise of her own heart at this moment. She isn't cold now. The blood is circulating in her veins again. A huge fatigue sweeps over her. She feels bound to the girl as never before, and at the same time hopelessly separate from her. Before she gives in to sleep, she wonders where the worn-out hearts of transplant patients go to rot.

You don't know if you should laugh or cry at this conclusion. You know it's the miracle that for days, even weeks, the thin little woman in the flowered dress had waited for.

"Courage is a telephone," she tells herself again and again, almost angrily. The week-long interval is nearly over. It's eleven p.m. by the cathedral clock and Friday on the calendar. The work week has just ended. He must be getting ready to leave, if he hasn't already. Clutched in her fist is the ravaged scrap of paper. All week she's been complaining about the trap he set by giving her the advantage of making the first move. She's annoyed with him for not showing up at the café when she's gone there practically every day; he could have taken pity on her and called, he has her name and address, there's such a thing as a phone book. He's the shrink, after all, he could have made an effort.

She's afraid she's waited too long. What do you say to a man you hardly know when you call him at eleven p.m. when time is up? If she doesn't know what to say to a man at eleven p.m., she won't know any better at midnight or one a.m. Above all, she mustn't be seen for what she is: lonely and paralysed and clumsy.

She picks up the receiver and punches in the number. Because, if she doesn't, it will be like her loneliness on caviar. And she hates caviar, it makes her sick.

The girl has entered her room as if it were a sanctuary. Let herself fall onto the bed in one light movement, arms extended. It's the move she didn't make on the wharf a while ago. Now she knows what the answer is. It will be a matter of going on. In what way, in what condition? She doesn't know, she hasn't made any decisions. Inside her body, unbeknownst to her, this day has been engraved. Like the piercing eyes of the enormous, curious rat that came silently to feed very close to her. In a moment, the animal decided what would come next. The girl thinks that she was wrong about the future, that it takes on the most amazing shape when you least expect it. The future is a rat that terrorizes without knowing it. Perhaps the desire to live stems quite simply from the revulsion aroused by a rat advancing along the beam under a dock. Hugging her childhood teddy bear, about to give in to sleep, she thinks that perhaps the ultimate affection could be that too: a dirty rat in the night that stares at her as if urging her not to go beyond the far edge of the wharf.

In the morning the two of you still haven't left. You have
not yet got to the bottom of their truth. You have to take
away two or three secrets they haven't revealed to you.
On this first morning of summer a strong wind, warm
and damp, sends the usual salty odours over the town.
Summer is entering their lives through the front door.

You don't have much time. That wind has come up
for you. It will be your second raft.

You've taken off across town so the population can
turn over to you this thing that you'll never possess, that
you've refused but that they're keeping safe in the palms
of their hands: their future.

You went first of all to the farthest edge of town, to
the end of a narrow street that looks down on the river.
In the bedroom upstairs, the dark sleep of the thin little
woman whose future is the pain that pulls her out of
bed every day. In a while, she'll open her eyes to the
same image as every morning. A schoolbus carrying two
young boys she'll never see again. And to another lost
image. The last kiss, the last time her hand stroked your
hair, the last sign of an affection that wasn't enough. Later
this morning she'll go downtown, go into stores where
no one knows her. She'll smile at the cashier, talk about
the warm wind, about the return of summer. Nothing
will show. Even the worst doesn't kill you. You don't
rebuild yourself either. She'll buy food that will keep her
alive. You won't be at ease with that future. You'll follow her on the road home. Go around the house one last

time. Behind, leaning against the wall just under the little woman's bedroom window, your raft. Like a slowly rotting grave facing the river. On the clothesline, the little flowered dress that the wind snaps and will carry away in a moment. A minuscule sign. A hope.

Then you went back towards the centre of town, you took a street that climbs as it moves away from the river. You stopped at a car that was parked under the trees. On the back seat were piled boxes and clothing. Last night at eleven, a man had finished packing. He'd decided to move out at dawn. He was leaving nothing behind but his signature at the bottom of some medical files. In the one-room furnished apartment he'd rented for six months, all he'd kept for the night were his alarm clock and two beers. He'd flung the window wide open, and wondered when he saw his car if it might not be better to leave now and travel at night.

The future is first of all silence at the end of the line, and then, in a superhuman effort, the toneless voice of a woman who hasn't prepared what she'll say, doesn't even know what will emerge from her mouth when the man says for the second time, "Yes?" The future is a man at eleven-thirty p.m., at the wheel of a car filled with luggage. He won't set out on his trip tonight. In this town that he doesn't know well, he's looking for a tree-lined street where a woman lives who hasn't asked him to stay, just to come over.

The future is an open window in a bedroom, a warm, damp wind that trickles in, the pallor of dawn. It is this room like a raft that's slowly coming back to shore. A sleeping man, the whiteness of the sheets, his arm folded over his face.

He won't leave for a while. He'll wait for the Sunday

evening traffic to go back home. Throughout the trip he'll
have a growing certainty that he'll travel this road often,
in both directions.

She watches him sleep. The night has been easy.
That's what was needed to hook the beginning of a story
to her life. She doesn't move for fear of waking the man
who's asleep at her side, for fear that the image will disappear, just as the image of the two of you disappeared
from the mirror one fine or not so fine morning, she's
not sure which.

You've come up to the bed. You've seen them somewhere else, later on, in another town, bigger and greyer.
You've seen her resist, explain that she won't come, that
it's out of the question for her to leave the place where
she's always lived, where she works. You've noticed in
particular that every time the man says "my son" or, even
worse, "my child," the pain deep in his eyes reappears
and strengthens her refusal to join him.

You've also seen him say no every time she insists
on going with him when he visits his son.

Then, no doubt from fear of losing her, he finally gave
in. You followed them one Sunday afternoon, down the
white, faded corridors. You saw a frail young man, broken, with a life expectancy of no more than twenty years,
his wandering gaze, his dislocated movements, his fingers those of a child, his fine hair.

Something she'd never had was given back to her.

Shortly after, you saw her on the highway that follows the river upstream, moving away from the town
she'd never left, in a car full of luggage.

The future is a dog, a sort of hero for the day, who goes in and out as he pleases, through a torn screen door. The boys egg him on with shrill little cries. First day of summer holidays, a warm wind enters the bright kitchen.

The two of you have come to brush against them one last time.

She woke at dawn, still wrapped in the woollen blanket on the living-room sofa. Stiff and sore. She put on her watch, put the blanket away. There won't be any traces. She's gone back to the kitchen and repeated the familiar acts. The coffee, the orange juice on the table, the toast. It's a morning like any other.

The phone rings. She hears her hoarse, tired voice say no, there was no emergency, she'd just wanted to know if he'd had a good trip. She asks when he's coming home. Talks loudly because of the boys and the dog. Hangs up saying, See you tomorrow.

Automatically she folds her old bathrobe over her chest. Today she'll buy another one. Slow movements in the kitchen, this day is trying to settle in.

The overexcited dog finally gets stuck in the screen door. His head and forepaws in the kitchen, the rest of his body outside. Whines. The boys howl with delight.

She bursts out laughing.

She has turned around, drawn by a presence behind her. The girl in the kitchen. A hint of a smile at the dog's performance. Her pallor. The fragility of the world and of love. Their eyes meet. She'll never ask for an accounting.

Will never try to find out what did or didn't happen. Just one thing to hold onto: in the girl's smile something is trying to live. A tenuous thread. That will do for an answer.

Just before leaving them, you touched the girl's cheek. For the time being she isn't trying to understand. The blisters on her feet hurt. That's what is left of her journey: those little wounds no one will notice. She thinks that when they've gone, nothing of the journey will survive. She doesn't know yet that for the rest of her life everything she does will bear the mark of this day. That even at the most transparent moments, when she says words filled with the future, when she walks, dazzled, in a vast city on another continent, when arm-in-arm with a man she sometimes throws back her head and laughs, she'll never move away from the very end of the docks.

A day like the others. With its cries and its secrets. The kitchen's empty now. The dog has led the boys outside, the girl has gone back up to her room. An awkward squirrel has hopped onto the narrow windowsill. He's hanging on as best he can. The two of them look at each other. She in her old bathrobe, he in his damp fur. The future is terra firma.

Around noon the wind has calmed down. Out at sea the last clouds have disappeared. On all sides, the blue has started to strike again. You've gone. We didn't even turn our heads. For a moment we stood there motionless, silent, staring vacantly out at the river. Then we resumed our robot-like little habits. Nonchalant, anonymous, without memory.

We smile, our tongues are untied. In cafés and stores the sounds of clinking glasses, shouts and music begin to mark the beat of this town's pulse again. Gangs of boys and girls bike to the sandbars. Children take over the playgrounds. The enlargement of the marina, geraniums planted in the public parks, the arrival of colonies of ducks near the shores make the front page of the local paper. The mourning is over.

You've gone. We didn't even turn our heads to follow the course of the river. You took away everything. Suddenly the world looked bigger to us, the future broader. It seems as if we're coming home after a war to a devastated but familiar place. Never again will we repeat your names. We tremble when one of us utters the word "promises" or "plans." We're still fragile but we don't want to admit it.

And so we walk along the banks of the river now, at the beginning of summer, and we believe that we've been healed.